# "You realize we are now engaged?"

Blue eyes cold as ice chips viewed her defiance unmoved. "You've handed yourself to me on a platter, my dear."

"Break it," Sian urged caustically. "You have no wish to be engaged to me."

"On the personal note, no—but I don't throw away golden opportunities. You might remember that the next time you throw out a challenge."

"Oh, I will," she declared fiercely, eyes burning. "Believe me, I will. So what are you going to do?"

He grinned. "I'm glad you have a temper. I never did like passive women." He reached out a hand and traced the line of her lips. "I promise you'll be first to know what I decide. I'll think of something appropriate. It won't hurt you to stew about it for the weekend."

**Amanda Browning** is a new British author who lives in Essex. She is single, and a former librarian.

**Books by Amanda Browning**

HARLEQUIN PRESENTS
1055—PERFECT STRANGERS

Don't miss any of our special offers. Write to us at the following address for information on our newest releases.

Harlequin Reader Service
901 Fuhrmann Blvd., P.O. Box 1397, Buffalo, NY 14240
Canadian address: P.O. Box 603,
Fort Erie, Ont. L2A 5X3

# The Asking Price
## Amanda Browning

*Harlequin Books*

TORONTO • NEW YORK • LONDON
AMSTERDAM • PARIS • SYDNEY • HAMBURG
STOCKHOLM • ATHENS • TOKYO • MILAN

Original hardcover edition published in 1988
by Mills & Boon Limited

ISBN 0-373-03031-2

Harlequin Romance first edition February 1990

# CHAPTER ONE

SIAN THOMAS had her nose firmly entrenched in a newspaper when the lift in which she was ascending came to a sudden and unscheduled stop somewhere between the ninth and tenth floors. Two things conspired to make her see red. Firstly, her fellow passengers had, as usual, debouched on the lower floors, leaving her alone. Added to which, this was the second time in as many days that she had found herself trapped.

It was the last straw! She hadn't been blessed with red hair for nothing, even if it was at this moment hidden from sight beneath a shaggy fur hat. Her temper, already on a short rein after a less than happy start to the day, bubbled over into fury. It didn't happen often, but when it did, it had all the spectacular effects of a firework display.

The paper became airborne and her handbag bounced off the wall with a loud metallic clang as she flung it to the floor. Then with simultaneous movements she aimed a kick at the recalcitrant door and the flat of her palm to the control panel.

The result was stunning: everything went pitch-black, and into the darkness rang a deep, throaty, vastly amused chuckle.

Sian's heart leapt into her throat and she spun round like a top, losing her balance slightly and almost shrieking in alarm when her steadying hand came into contact with something warm and soft to the touch.

'God!' she gasped, fright taking most of her voice away.

'Close, but not strictly accurate.' The softly drawled words came to her out of the darkness, their tone rich and vibrantly male.

In a dizzying wave of vertigo, Sian's mind resurrected the knowledge that the devil lived in darkness, and it seemed to her she had dredged him up from her deepest, darkest nightmares. For she knew that voice.

Knew its nicety of inflexion as it expressed anger and contempt. Her mind drew forth the picture of a dark-haired man standing on the far side of a grave, his face cold and harsh and unforgiving. She shivered.

'Where did you come from?' Though she tried to control it, her voice carried the high-pitched thread of alarm.

She felt the hesitation before the voice went on in the same mildly humorous tone. 'Something tells me if I make a joke about coming from outer space, I might get more than I bargained for. The truth is very simple—I was here all the time.'

Sian heard him out, her heart knocking so painfully fast against the wall of her chest that she had to press a hand to it. Relief invaded her stricken mind. He didn't know her. Apart from that small hesitation, there had been no recognition of her own voice in his. A strangled sob was caught by grimly tensed lips. After all these years, some monstrous quirk of fate had set her down here, trapped in a lift with Blair Davenport, the one man she had, with anger and despair, hoped never to see again.

Their acquaintance had been brief but virulent, and she had never forgotten it, nor his voice. Yet he seemed to have done so, and that very fact would help her survive this incarceration—if she could only pretend he was a stranger, too.

The disembodied voice broke into her thoughts. 'Are you about to panic? I ask merely because my head won't be too happy if I have to deal with a case of hysterics.' There was a droll touch of humour there, directed at himself.

Sian had to clench her fists until her nails scored her palms to respond to that casually. 'If you're asking me if I suffer from claustrophobia, then the answer is no. You're quite safe.'

'Thank you,' he replied humbly.

For all his mild manner, or maybe because of it, her inner tension rapidly became unbearable. Oh, God, hurry up and get me out of here, she prayed a shade hysterically. To remain in silence was insupportable, and she cast about wildly for something to say to break it.

'Do you think I caused the lights to go out, or was it a coincidence?'

'Your thumps looked pretty efficient, and against someone like me, in my sensitive condition, you'd probably do a grand job, but these lifts were designed to take harder blows than yours. I don't think you need worry about a law suit for criminal damage this time.' There was a definite teasing note to the voice that sent a shiver along her spine.

'Do you think they'll take long to get us out? Should I ring the alarm bell?' She took her cue from him.

'It no doubt escaped your notice, but you did that already with your karate chop.'

'Oh!'

'Quite,' the voice drawled drily. 'As to how long, I couldn't say. I only hope it's sooner than later. I need some aspirin.'

This was the third time he had mentioned his head, and although her strongest instinct was to invite no revelations of a personal nature, Sian was unable to ignore it any longer.

'Bad night?' she queried jerkily.

'One damn drink after another,' he groaned morosely.

In spite of her circumstances she laughed, a light bell of sound that echoed in the enclosed space. 'You ought to know better.'

'Tell my brother that. It was his stag night. Thank God he chose to have it yesterday. When I left him he was pretty green about the gills. In no state to get married today.' He sounded as sympathetic as a man in a similar condition could be.

At that point, and with a suddenness as blinding as the previous Stygian gloom, the lighting came back on. Sian heard the groan as the brightness sent pain arrowing through her companion, but her thoughts were elsewhere. She hadn't taken this eventuality into consideration when she had set out to pretend they were strangers. Her voice he might forget, but she didn't imagine for a minute he wouldn't recognise her face. Her hair, that tell-tale mass of vibrant deep-red locks, was hidden, it was true, but how could she hide her face? With something like desperation she remembered the newspaper. If she turned her shoulder and buried herself in it again, he might never know who he had shared his captivity with. It was the work of a moment to put the plan into operation.

'Sian, darling, you may be tall, but the resemblance to an ostrich ends there,' the voice declared humorously, only there was an edge to it now that had been missing before.

Her heart lurched painfully. The newspaper fluttered from her nerveless fingers as she turned towards him, scarcely daring to breathe. Pride, and a self-control born of necessity, hid whatever reaction she felt to seeing Blair Davenport face to face for the first time in five years.

He was leaning against the wall of the lift, arms folded across his chest, and his feet crossed at the ankles, giving the impression of being totally at ease. The first thought that struck her was that he was as handsome as ever, even though he looked distinctly the worse for wear the morning after the night before. Thick waves of black hair framed the strong, masculine face, curling temptingly over his collar. There was a sallow tinge beneath the lean, tanned cheeks and a puffiness around his eyes, but even that couldn't hide the strength there. Nor did it disguise in any way the sensual curve of his mouth.

She dragged air into her lungs shakily. Behind the cool mask which was her face, every outraged sensibility took in the look of him. She felt the abrupt tightening of her stomach muscles as she familiarised herself with the catlike grace he wore so naturally. He was, at thirty-five, a sleek male animal, ready to leap into action at a moment's notice. Her reaction to him, unwanted and unexpected, came as the severest shock. Deplore it as she might, her feminine core was stirred by his maleness. Yet, in the same way you might admire a tiger, you couldn't forget it was dangerous.

Now, of all moments, she needed her wits about her.

'Hello, Blair. Its been a long time.'

His teeth flashed in a smile. 'Indeed it has. But what is it they say? Time has no meaning between old friends,' he returned amicably.

She recognised the irony and a little colour stole into her cheeks. 'What do they say about old enemies?'

He gave that some thought, blue eyes glittering through narrowed lids. 'I imagine that in a war where soldiers have lost all sense of the reason for the fight, meeting an old adversary must feel like meeting an old friend,' he pronounced at last, then added, 'After that, they try to kill each other.'

She was too intelligent to miss the allusion, and she flinched as the words struck home. He saw it and smiled. Deep inside her a hope died, stillborn. He hadn't forgotten or forgiven. Instinctively she donned the robes of the part she had set herself five years ago.

Her sardonic smile was an impressive thing under the circumstances. 'Why did you pretend not to know me just now?' she mocked.

'Why did you?' he countered smoothly. 'Shall we say, it appealed to my sense of the ridiculous. I was intrigued as to what you would do, and surprise, surprise, you did nothing. Why was that? Guilt, perhaps?'

Another dart found its vulnerable mark. She laughed lightly. 'I have nothing to be guilty about.' She shrugged, and made herself relax against the wall. 'What did you want me to do?'

She watched his mouth twist in a broad smile that failed to reach his dark blue eyes. 'It might have been nice if you had flung yourself into my arms with fond cries of joy, and perhaps a tear or two,' he said unkindly.

The glaring electric light hid the fact that she paled. 'That would have been expecting too much.'

Blair laughed this time. 'I rather think I got the reception I was expecting. After all, there's no point pretending now, is there? So, tell me, how are you?'

'Very well, as always. And you?'

The gambit made him smile thinly. 'Thriving. I can see you've done well for yourself. What is it, marriage or a rich lover?'

'Neither, just a fair wage for a good day's work.' She ignored his gibe, but it was hard.

'Really? You do surprise me. I thought for Daddy's little girl, that was much too demeaning,' he goaded, eyes flashing blue sparks.

Sian's stomach twisted into a knot, and she breathed deeply to hold on to her temper. It was what he wanted, for her to lose control. She couldn't allow him the victory. 'You're right, of course, but I'm also my mother's daughter, and that girl works for her living.'

'And you've been here—what, six months?' he pursued casually.

She couldn't control a gasp that time. 'How did you know?'

He held her gaze steadily. 'I always keep my finger on the pulse of my companies.'

This was the harshest blow yet to fall on her hapless shoulders. She had thought he was only visiting. '*Your* company?' she asked faintly. 'I didn't know.'

'I took the company over less than a year ago. Part of the agreement was to leave old Fielding where he was until he retired. Which, as you know, he has just done.

Now I take over his seat, visibly, as it were,' he informed her.

Sian swallowed. 'I see.'

'Going to cut and run now you know?' Blair enquired mockingly.

She gathered her retreating composure like a cloak. She couldn't let him see how this news unnerved her. 'Hardly. You pay far too well, and I enjoy my work.'

'I'm glad to hear it,' he said grimly. 'Because I would not have liked to take you to court for breach of contract.'

'It would have been petty, even for you,' she agreed silkily, her heart thudding so hard that it nearly choked her.

Silence reigned in the aftermath of that exchange, and Blair used it to take lazy stock of her. Sian shivered as the blue eyes inspected her openly, and witnessed the upturn of his lips as he caught her reaction. She could only stand locked to the spot as he took his time taking in every inch of her. From the delicate bones of her face and their fine covering of skin the colour and texture of porcelain, his gaze swept slowly past large blue eyes framed by long, dark lashes, to the trembling fullness of her lips. All this before sweeping downwards over the hidden curves of her body to her long, shapely legs.

With a last look, Blair straightened up, flexing his muscles, showing her clearly the strong legs and powerful shoulders in his close-fitting grey suit. She drew herself up into a tautly controlled figure as he crossed the small space that separated them, to stand before her. His arm came out, and in one smooth movement, while her heart took up an anxious knocking, her hat was plucked from her head and discarded, to be replaced by hands combing their way through the crowning glory of her hair.

'Neal always used to say he could bask in this warmth for a lifetime and consider the world well lost. He's lost to the world now, anyway,' he mused, allowing the liquid fire to run through his fingers.

Sian caught her breath as the questing caress of his fingers went on to probe beneath her hair, but her instinct to move away was halted on a wince as his fingers tightened, holding her captive. She swallowed convulsively as her heart leapt into her throat, and her stomach lurched on a wave of dread.

Blair was still studying her hair with an absorbed expression. 'Beautiful,' he said, and stepped back away from her. 'You always were. I always thought you showed promise. Neal's mistake was in trying to keep it all for himself.'

That recalled a pain only sheer bravado kept from showing on her face. 'I was no man's property,' she said disdainfully.

'We got that message a long time ago. You always had such a way with words. Direct and to the point,' he told her narrowly.

'Sour grapes, Blair?' she mocked.

He went on as if she hadn't spoken. 'You left so fast after the funeral, there wasn't time for me to talk to you. But I'll tell you now—this time you won't get away so easily.'

Sian managed to produce a scornful laugh. 'You always had a monumental conceit. There isn't going to be a this time.'

Like two contenders they faced up to each other. 'You think not? Time will tell, won't it, my darling? A word of warning, Sian, in case you've forgotten. I never make idle threats.'

This time she came away from the wall in an angry movement. 'You have no right to threaten me.'

'Poor, foolish Neal isn't here to do it for himself, is he? He was like a brother to me, and I take what you did personally.'

'I never intended it to end that way.' She made a despairing bid for his understanding, biting her lip when she saw she had failed.

It drew his eyes as surely as a magnet. 'Did Neal ever tell you, you have an eminently kissable mouth?'

A painful wave of memories assaulted her, of shared kisses and laughter. Of his words of praise lingering in her ears. Anguish fuelled anger, and restored her to the role she must play. Only she couldn't look at him. 'He was blessed with a golden tongue. I believe he must have mentioned it. I didn't really pay much attention.'

'It's not important.' He shrugged. 'You were a girl then, but you're a woman now. An experienced one too, I don't doubt. It will be an interesting experiment, discovering if the substance lives up to the promise,' he declared provocatively.

Sian's nerves fluttered at the thinly veiled statement of intent. The last thing she needed was for him to kiss her. The torture she suffered now would be as nothing to that. But how to avoid it? 'Hardly original, wouldn't you say? I have no desire for your kisses,' she said, but he wasn't listening.

'I used to hear chapter and verse about your kisses from Neal, especially when he was drinking. It made me wonder just what they were like. How they could drive a sane man like him to ruin.'

She drew a hasty breath, then controlled it quickly. 'Well, you can keep on wondering. I've grown rather discriminating about whom I kiss these days.'

Blair shook his head reprovingly. 'Bitchiness doesn't become you.'

Sian folded her arms. Mockery wouldn't work, but perhaps scorn would. 'I really don't care if what I do or say pleases you. As far as I'm concerned you're just another self-satisfied, second-rate Casanova. You always were and you always will be.'

His eyes became a bright glittering blue, but his smile came quite breathtakingly into the open as he mocked back, 'Why, darling, what a quaintly old-fashioned term to use. I would have expected a far more emasculating description of what you think of me.'

She laughed, but it sounded brittle to her own ears. 'Don't tempt me.'

Blair's eyes narrowed to speculative slits. 'I wonder if I could? After all, I'm worth more than Neal these days.'

Shock made her nerves leap in every centimetre of skin. Pain struck the defences from her, leaving her open and starkly vulnerable. Had it not been for the sudden eruption of furious activity echoing down to them from above, she might even have screamed. Clearly it wouldn't be too long before they were released. More than anything, Sian wanted to escape this prison. Every minute she spent with Blair was peeling away her protective covering, revealing her, naked and assailable to the hurt she had once suffered. Her tension transmitted itself to him.

'Relax,' Blair's voice advised mildly. 'You'll soon be able to leave my—what was the delightful phrase Neal told me?—mediocre company, that was it.'

'I can't wait!' she sniped caustically. 'Tell me, did you intend for us to meet?'

'Of course. I always knew precisely where I could find you. I knew that one day I'd get the golden opportunity I wanted. The chance to talk over old times with you.'

The absolute certainty in his voice, the determination to claim an eye for an eye, made her shiver. Yet she managed to say, 'Rather boring, I should imagine.'

His smile was loaded with malice. 'I shall endeavour to make it interesting.'

The lift-cage jolted, but remained fixed.

'Shouldn't be too long now,' Blair said, and she wondered if he wanted to get out as badly as she did. But no, he was enjoying this.

'I can't say I'll be sorry,' she said drily.

Blair slanted her a glance, then took the two steps necessary to enclose her against the wall, an arm braced either side, blocking her escape.

'Nervous, darling?'

'No.'

His eyes glittered. 'You should be,' he advised softly.

Her heart quailed. 'Of you?' she mocked.

'Everything must be paid for, and you still owe.'

'I don't have any base coin on me,' she declared contemptuously.

He shrugged. 'No matter. I'll take payment in kind. A kiss from those lovely lips will do as a first instalment.'

Sian looked into remorseless eyes and couldn't breathe. She rallied her defences to fight him just as the small cubicle lurched into life, propelling her straight into the arms she had hoped to avoid. Blair wasn't slow to take advantage of a heaven-sent opportunity. His arms caught her against him while his head swooped to claim her lips with his.

Sian bore the onslaught with tears glistening along her lashes, tears that couldn't be allowed to fall. All his anger and contempt were contained in that bruising pressure. He made free of what she tried to deny him with a sensual mastery that degraded in its lack of real desire. Yet that wasn't all. With a silent scream she felt her senses start to swim, and her lips to answer the command of his. Desperation added strength, and she fought free of his hold. Blair didn't attempt to stop her, and she soon found out why.

To her horror she discovered that, while she had been conscious of nothing but his kiss, the lift had carried them up to the next floor, and the rescue party, plus interested onlookers, had been rewarded with the sight of her locked in Blair Davenport's arms when the lift door finally opened.

You could have heard a pin drop. With studied gallantry, Blair retrieved her hat, bag and paper and restored them to her, smiling sardonically at her rigid figure.

'Thank you,' he murmured, for her ears only. 'Now I know. I'll be in touch.' Then he stepped out, clapping a hand on the maintenance man's shoulder as he passed. 'Your timing was a bit out there, Mac.'

Mac grinned, showing his lack of teeth proudly. 'Sure was, Mr D. I'll do better next time.'

'You do that.'

Sian watched them all grinning at his departing back, and it was clear they all thought him a proper Jack-the-lad. With head held high and viciously muttered 'excuse me's, she cleared a path for herself to the stairs in Blair's wake, but for her it was like running the gauntlet. The sound of their speculation followed her up the stairs. In less than an hour, she knew, it would be all over the building.

She escaped into her office and shut the door. Dropping her belongings haphazardly on her desk, she collapsed into her chair and rested her head on her hands.

Oh, why had she had to run into Blair? He reminded her of Neal and all she had hoped to forget. He wouldn't let her, she knew that. She remembered his face as she had seen it last, across the yawning maw of the grave, and there had been no forgiveness in it, only a promise of retribution.

She hadn't wanted Neal to die. She had loved him. Only Blair would never believe that. Not with the way she had treated him.

Neal Fellowes. She had met him the summer she came down from university. He was several years older than her, witty, charming, rather boyish in an endearing sort of way. She had fallen in love with him before she knew it. Maybe he hadn't been strong, but he had been kind and generous, and fun. Life had been full of promise. They had happily made plans for the future.

Only there hadn't been a future for her and Neal. Her father had seen to that. She hadn't accepted until then just exactly what kind of man he was. Sir Rhodri had been a strict, uncompromising man as she grew up. She didn't remember her mother at all, for she had died when Sian was very small. Her father had packed her off to boarding-school as soon as possible, and she had seen very little of him over the years. As a youngster, it had hurt that he didn't love her as she expected him to. Older, it had turned life into a battlefield, as she had fought his indifference and demands of blind obedience. Despite the hostilities, she had never truly believed he would ride roughshod over her. That had been a revelation of the worst kind.

It hadn't mattered to him who she was, nor that she loved Neal. He had issued his orders. She was not to see Neal again. Of course, she had railed against that, sure that he would come round in the end. Then one day he had issued her an ultimatum. She had refused to credit it without an explanation. He hadn't given her one, but he had told her what he would do if she didn't agree. He had information that would destroy Neal, his business and his family. Because she was his daughter he was prepared not to use it, upon condition. He would not have his daughter allying herself with a family he considered to be his bitterest enemy.

Sian hadn't doubted he would do as he threatened. And Neal would find out it had been her father who had made it happen. How long would his love last then? Her father had had her trapped and he knew it. At least if she did what her father wanted, Neal would be left with something.

So she had done it.

Even now it made her shudder to remember it. She had broken off with Neal that very night. Long afterwards she had had nightmares in which she saw his face etched with disbelief and pain. She hadn't been prepared for him not to give up. He would turn up day and night to plead with her until she had had to say awful things and laugh in his face to get him to go away. She

hadn't seen him after that, but she had heard through
a friend that he was drinking heavily—and then one day
he was dead. He had driven his car into a wall.

It didn't help to know he had been drunk at the time,
because she had known she was the cause of it. She had
wanted to run away then, but she had forced herself to
stay till after the funeral. Besides, she had known she
could never run away from the guilt.

That was when she had seen Blair for the second and
last time. They hadn't spoken. Everything that had had
to be said had been voiced when he'd called on her before
Neal died. He had only been a name to her before. Neal's
friend who was in the States. He had come back to find
his friend in the state she had unwillingly brought him
to.

He had called on her one evening, demanding to know
why she had treated his friend so cavalierly. Already
crumpling under the weight of her guilt, the only way
to bear this new attack was to don the cloak of a callous,
wilfully spoilt girl, and repeat the lies she had told Neal.
Blair's contempt had seared her but she had lifted her
chin in defiance. He had left abruptly, never to know
that she had barely waited for the door to close behind
him, to rush to her room and break down.

She had left home the day after the funeral; she hadn't
been able to live under the same roof as her father. She
would never forgive him for what he had made her do.
She had come south and made a new life for herself. It
hadn't been easy, but the hard work had been a kind of
therapy. Yet she couldn't have foretold that she would
one day find herself at Fielding's—in Blair Davenport's
clutches.

Sian sat back in her seat and looked at her hands.
They were shaking. She wasn't surprised.

Blair had issued veiled threats that she knew couldn't
be ignored. What was he going to do? He wouldn't leave
her in peace, she knew that. She couldn't live with this
unknown something hanging over her head. She had to

know, to be prepared. This time she couldn't run. She had a home, a career, a whole way of life she loved.

Impotently she clenched her hands into fists. It was all such a terrible, impossible mess. Sheer bravado had made her act that way in the lift, yet she knew the impression she must have given—totally selfish and unrepentant. That wasn't true, but she couldn't change it now. Heavens, she felt so helpless. Like a mouse the cat allowed to run only so far before swatting back with a practised flick of a paw.

The buzz of the intercom made her jump violently. Pulling herself together, she reached for the switch.

'Yes, Mr Wheatley?'

'What's keeping you, Sian?' a testy voice replied. 'You should have brought the post in ages ago.'

Sian rolled her eyes. 'Yes, I know. I'm sorry. I got caught in the lift again. I'll bring it through directly.'

There was nothing for it, Blair had to be put to the back of her mind while she got on with her job. Mr Wheatley was head of sales at Fielding's. She had been working for him for six months, and he had always expressed himself well satisfied with her. Yet she wouldn't have been surprised if her performance that day caused him to sack her on the spot. Her usual efficiency went to pot, and she seemed to be all fingers and thumbs. She was immensely relieved when the hands of the clock finally crawled round towards five.

She was busily finishing a letter, referring to the screen of the computer beside her for information, when an idea occurred to her, and her fingers fluttered to a halt on the typewriter keys. Glancing back at the computer, she bit her lip. The console gave her access to all sorts of information—like personnel files. Blair would be on it, and his address. If she had that, she could go and see him and demand to know what he was going to do.

Seconds later she had the address written on a piece of paper, and her heart was already thundering madly at the idea of setting foot in his domain. Of course, the alternative would be to see him in his office, but that would be all round the building in five minutes flat. The less people who knew she had business with Blair, the better.

It wasn't a meeting she looked forward to, but then, the situation wasn't one she had ever expected to find herself in. Neal and that terrible time was something she had hoped was behind her, but Blair had other ideas.

Well, bad news, like bad medicine, had to be taken quickly. She would go tonight. Once she knew, she could decide what she was going to do. She had told him she wasn't going to leave, but she wasn't cut out to be a masochist. If it seemed the better option, she would take it.

She did some necessary shopping on the way home. When she did get in, it was already getting late, so she made herself a slice of cheese on toast and a cup of tea, and then hurried into her bedroom to change her dress.

Seven o'clock that evening found her ringing the doorbell of his apartment. He was clearly expecting someone when he answered the door, but it wasn't her—as his sudden stillness proclaimed.

'Well, well, this *is* a surprise. The wild horses too strong for you, were they?' he drawled with heavy irony.

Sian bristled but held her temper. 'May I come in?'

His brows rose as he stood back. 'Please do. I'm intrigued by this sudden desire for my company.' Shutting the door behind him with a small click—which nevertheless sounded like the clanging to of a cell door—he led the way into the lounge.

There was a news programme on the television, but he switched it off. He turned to her then, watching silently as she stared about her.

'Does it take your fancy?'

'It's cold,' she answered bluntly. The decoration and furniture were the best, but whoever had chosen them had added very little warmth. It wasn't a place you wanted to rush home to.

Blair looked about him too. 'Hmm, my mother agrees with you. She says it reminds her of charity. Dee wasn't amused.'

A little disconcerted by his amiability, Sian took a deep breath. 'Actually, I didn't come here to talk about furniture.'

'Nor you did,' he agreed sardonically. 'Why don't you take your coat off and sit down? Can I get you something to drink?'

On the point of refusing, she changed her mind and asked for a sherry. He poured a whisky for himself and then sat down on the couch facing her.

'Now, what can I do for you?' he enquired as if his one mission in life was to fulfil her every wish.

Her apprehension erupted into a nervous outburst. 'You make it sound like a social occasion!'

His brows rose. 'I can be as unpleasant as you want in the blink of an eye, but I can assure you, you wouldn't like it. Suffice it to say, I was brought up to be polite to guests—welcome or unwelcome,' he told her amicably, his eyes as cold as ice. 'So why don't you say what you've come to say?'

Brought up short, she licked her lips. This was worse than she'd expected. 'Today you . . . you seemed to imply . . .'

'Only seemed?' he laughed, and sipped at his drink. 'Go on.'

'Implied,' she went on hardily, 'that you would take some form of retaliation for what happened five years ago. I want to know what you intend to do,' she finished on a note of challenge.

Blair studied his glass, rolling it between his hands. 'Ah! Who was it? The Mikado? I'd say he had it right— to make the punishment fit the crime. What would you say was fitting, Sian?' He sent her a look of derision.

'I don't know,' she replied, looking away, too choked to return his scorn.

His hand reached out, framing and lifting her face. His touch was warm, but it struck chill to her very bones. His lip curled. 'Where's all that fine disdain now? It's different when you're afraid, isn't it? When you know you're going to be called to account.'

Jerking free, Sian set her glass down, its contents practically untouched. 'Are you going to tell me?' Her voice was unbearably wobbly.

'You know, I don't believe I would if I could. So it's rather fortunate for you that I don't know yet. I'll think of something, never fear.'

Her legs felt none too sure as she jumped to her feet. 'You're enjoying this, aren't you?'

Blair smiled. 'What do you think?' he asked, quietly but effectively.

In disarray Sian gathered up her coat and bag. 'Then there's no point in my staying any longer, is there?'

Blair came to his feet. 'None at all. I'll show you out.' His politeness was intimidating.

They were almost at the front door when the bell went. When Blair opened it, a slim, leggy blonde in her late twenties drifted into his arms, surrounding him in a cloud of Opium.

'Here I am, darling, did you miss me?' She lifted her face for his kiss and, as she did so, saw Sian for the first time. 'Who's this?' she demanded suspiciously.

Blair took one look at Sian's tight face and grinned. 'An old friend. She's just going, Dee.'

The blonde perked up, running her fingers provocatively down his cheek. 'Good. Get rid of her quickly, darling—we have a whole week to make up for.' Moving past him, she tossed Sian a haughty look and disappeared inside.

'The decorator?' Sian couldn't help dripping the question with sarcasm.

He just grinned. 'She more than makes up for it in other ways.'

'Aren't you the lucky one!'

'Goodnight, Sian,' he chuckled. 'I'll be in touch. That's a promise.'

She heard the door close as she walked away. She wished now that she hadn't come. Not only had it been a waste of time, but it had shown him just how worried she was. No wonder he had been so charming; he had known he had her on the run the second he saw her at his door. Dear heavens, all she had done was play right into his hands!

# CHAPTER TWO

SIAN made her way to work next day without any enthusiasm. She hadn't slept well, which made her head feel like a lead weight. All she had done yesterday was make mistakes, the sort Blair would capitalise on. The thought of having to carry on as normal while waiting for the axe to fall had done nothing for her appetite or her mood.

Entering her office, she removed her coat and hung it on the stand, then settled down at her desk to go through the post. She had scarcely picked up the letter opener when Mr Wheatley popped his head around the door.

'You'd better leave that, Sian. You're wanted upstairs. Mr Davenport's office.'

She stared at him with a sinking heart. 'Do you know why?'

'I do, but it's not for me to say. Mr Davenport wants to see you immediately you arrive. You'd better not keep him waiting.'

Sian pushed back her chair and stood up. This was it, then. She supposed she should be grateful he wasn't making her stew, which was frankly what she expected. Giving Mr Wheatley a falsely confident smile, she walked out into the corridor again.

The lift whisked her up to the top floor faster than she found comfortable. Outside his office she paused to smooth down the skirt of her dress and run a hand over her hair to make sure it sat silkily. Taking a deep breath, she knocked briskly.

'Come in.'

Blair's voice sounded abrupt through the intervening wood. Sian nevertheless took a firm hold of the door-handle and let herself in.

'You wanted to see me,' she said huskily, halting just inside the door.

Blair straightened up from a table littered with blue-prints, computer print-outs and various assorted papers. 'Don't stand there. Come in and shut the door. That's one thing you can remember, I don't care for people who hover,' he ordered brusquely, going over to his desk and sitting down as Sian shut the door and walked forward. 'Sit down.'

Sian gritted her teeth. 'Thank you, but I'd prefer to stand.'

Blair's cold blue eyes fastened on her face. 'Take a seat, Sian, or do you want me to come round there and make you?'

One glance at his face was enough to tell her it wasn't a bluff.

Jerkily, she seated herself on the edge of the chair and watched the amusement flicker across his face.

'That's better,' he declared with satisfaction.

Her chin went up. 'All right, I'm sitting down. Now, please will you get to the point, so that I can leave?'

'I wouldn't advise you to continue with that attitude. You aren't talking to Neal now. I won't take it lying down. Spoilt brats aren't exactly my flavour of the month. Do I make myself clear?' he commanded cuttingly.

'Perfectly,' Sian replied tautly, wincing. 'But as I imagine I won't be employed here for very much longer, it hardly seems worth it.'

Blair sat back and crossed one long leg over the other. 'Is that what you think?' he asked in amusement. 'That I'm about to fire you?'

'What else?' she clipped out, eyes sparkling with resentment at his attitude.

He laughed. 'You couldn't be more wrong. As of this moment, Sian darling, you are my personal secretary.'

Her eyes widened. 'Oh, no!'

'Oh, yes,' Blair returned sardonically.

'What happened to your own secretary?' she demanded. He could hardly have been working without one.

'I don't have one. Fielding's retired when he did. I've been using a temp. This is the perfect solution.'

Sian shook her head vehemently. 'I work for Mr Wheatley, and I'm perfectly satisfied with things the way they are. I don't want this.'

Blair's face hardened visibly. 'It isn't a question of what *you* want, but what *I* want. That, darling, is to have you where I can keep an eye on you. I don't trust you, Sian. You ran away once, and I'm going to make sure you don't get the opportunity a second time. I've waited for this moment a long time. You may think you got away with murder, but you haven't. Now is the time you start to pay.'

Sian's whole body jolted at his choice of words. He thought she had been having fun, when all the time she was serving a life sentence!

'You're crazy if you think I'll stay here and let you walk all over me.'

Blue eyes gleamed. 'Oh, you'll stay, because I'll make sure there's nowhere else for you to go. Attempt to leave and I'll blacken your name from here to the ends of the earth. There may be jobs where you don't need references, but frankly, I can't see you sweeping the streets. You've been too spoilt. You've enjoyed the good life too long. Of course, you could prove me wrong.' He left that open, regarding her stricken features mockingly.

He had her in a corner and he knew it. He was enjoying watching her squirm. Well, she wasn't going to give him that satisfaction. She had paid in ways he couldn't even begin to imagine. She wasn't going to pay again.

'I'll need time to get my things together,' she said huskily.

If he had expected further argument, he hid his surprise well. 'I'm glad you're intelligent. We should work well together. I'll give you fifteen minutes.'

Sian was back in ten, and glad of it. Mr Wheatley had made quite a show of congratulating her on her good fortune in claiming the pick of jobs. It had been all she could do to smile and be polite, even though she knew it wasn't his fault. He introduced her to the girl who was taking her place. Sian vaguely remembered seeing her about. She passed on as much information as she could while she packed her personal items into a box, advising her to ring upstairs if she needed help.

Then it was time to go. Sian took one last look around, ostensibly for anything she might have left. She had been happy here. She didn't expect to enjoy her new domain. With a smile for her successor, she left. In the lift she sank wearily against the wall.

This whole business had been meticulously planned. It hadn't been done in half an hour. Blair must have set it in motion yesterday, which meant he had lied to her last night. His ruthlessness made her shiver. How on earth could she work with him under these circumstances? It would be soul-destroying. Yet she was trapped, unless she could think of a way out. She *must* think of one.

She found her new office without troubling Blair. It was light and spacious, with an interconnecting door. Although it was closed, she could feel Blair's presence on the other side, intimidating. Only she wasn't a weak mouse. She would fight him with all her strength of will.

Having settled that in her mind, Sian stowed her bits and pieces and turned to the stack of mail waiting for attention. In her work she was confident she wouldn't fall short. If he was expecting her to go to pieces, he had another think coming. She would work harder than

she had before, because she knew she would need to with
Blair, simply to stay on the same spot.

She worked smoothly, sorting as she went. In a drawer
she found folders obviously used by her predecessor,
slipped the piles inside and stood up. Catching up a pad
and pencil as she went, in case he had any instructions,
Sian crossed to the door, knocked once and went in.

Blair had removed his jacket and rolled up his shirt-
sleeves. He looked up from the papers he held, never
taking his eyes off her as she approached the desk.

Sian set the folders down. 'The mail. I've rough-sorted
it according to the labels on the folders as I don't know
if you have a routine you'd like me to follow,' she told
him briskly.

Setting aside the papers, he quickly flicked through
the pile before glancing up at her again. 'Very efficient,'
he drawled mockingly. 'Hoping to win me over? It will
take more than this.'

Sian bit down on a sharp reply. 'Not at all. If I have
to do this job, then I intend to do the best I can.'

'Highly commendable. If I have any complaints, I'll
be sure to let you know.'

She just bet he would!

'Right.' Blair sat back in his chair. 'There are a couple
of things you ought to know. I start work at eight and
go on until I'm ready to leave. I'll expect you to do the
same. You will, of course, be paid a salary commen-
surate with these hours.'

There was more in the same vein, and Sian listened
with a stolid face while he detailed her working life for
her. There was to be no easing into the new position.
She either sank or swam. Blair would love to see the
former, which strengthened her determination to do the
latter. When he had finished, he raised sardonic eyebrows in her direction.

'Any questions?'

'Why don't you just fix me up a camp bed in my office,
then I needn't go home at all? I do have a private life,

you know,' she couldn't help retorting sarcastically, and regretted it almost at once when his face clouded.

'Don't tell me there's another poor fool hanging around for the crumbs of your affection?' he jeered.

Sian gasped. 'I'm telling you no such thing.'

Blair went on as if she hadn't spoken. 'Well, whoever he is, I'm doing him a favour. Better this way than to have another wrecked life.'

Sian shot to her feet. 'That's enough!'

'Enough?' he scoffed. 'It's only the beginning. Before I'm through, you'll know yourself for what you are.'

She stood there, feeling the tremors inside and hoping they didn't show. 'Have you finished?'

He smiled grimly. 'For now. You can go. I'm sure you can find something to do. I'll buzz when I'm ready to do the mail.'

She escaped. There was no other word for it. With the door closed behind her, Sian sagged back weakly against it, shaking violently. If this was only the beginning, how much worse could it get? Her heart quailed for a moment, then she stiffened her spine and pushed herself upright. Of course it would get worse, but she mustn't let it get to her. He had no right to be judge, jury and executioner, whatever he believed, and it was up to her to deny him any sort of victory. At least visibly. For he could hurt her, he had that power, simply by preying on her own sense of guilt.

Sian gave herself a mental shake. She had to ignore it all as best she could and just do the job he expected of her. Which she did for the rest of the day, aided by the fact that Blair went out after lunch; and she didn't see him again before she left that evening.

She felt physically and mentally exhausted when she let herself into her small flat. She left hat, coat, bag and shoes variously across her lounge as she headed for her bathroom. She desperately needed to unwind, and a hot bath with lashings of bath salts would work wonders.

Minutes later she was sinking back into the water with a sigh of satisfaction. She wanted nothing more than to go to sleep, and that was the one thing she couldn't do. She could just imagine Blair's reaction if she failed to put in an appearance tonight.

Annually, Fielding's threw a St Valentine's Day dance, the proceeds of which were donated to charity. Though she wished it otherwise, tonight was the night. Everyone went to it unless they had a very good excuse. While she considered she had one, it was on the cards that Blair would notice her absence and put it down to cowardice.

Sian soaked as long as she dared before climbing out and getting herself ready. She had applied her make-up and was just stepping into her dress when the phone rang. She had a gut instinct for bad news even before she lifted the receiver. Ralph, her date for the evening, had developed 'flu and couldn't make it after all.

She made suitable commiserating noises even while she wanted to scream. Tonight was not the time for going to the party alone. That kiss yesterday was still on everyone's tongue, and attending unescorted was just asking for trouble. Apart from that, Ralph had been going to take her friend Sharon and her fiancé David in his car, too. Fortunately, when she rang Sharon it was to find David's car was out of dock again, so it was simple enough to arrange for them to pick her up instead of the other way around.

Sian finished dressing, wondering what else could go wrong today. There had already been two things, so there was bound to be a third.

The party was in full swing when they arrived and hunted out a table. Yet, despite the crowded dance-floor, Sian picked out Blair at once. He was dancing with a blonde and enjoying every minute of it. Following Sharon's back as they wove their way to a table, she decided that was fine. If he was occupied, he couldn't possibly favour her with one of his cutting comments.

As she sat down and looked about her, Sian hardly recognised the place. Someone had worked quite a transformation on the exhibition hall, for now it was decked out in a suitably romantic fashion, with any number of hearts and cupids floating from the ceiling. The lighting had been kept intimately low, with candles on every table adding to the atmosphere.

She did her best to join in as the party ebbed and flowed around her. She loved to dance, and the disco was excellent. However, she was acutely aware of the gossip. The kiss yesterday had set the wags wondering, and her sudden promotion today had added fuel to the fire. All her partners seemed interested in why she was alone, and if that meant there was some truth to the speculation surrounding herself and their employer. The fact that she had to keep to herself the knowledge she wouldn't touch him with a ten-foot barge-pole didn't help her humour.

After a particularly persistent encounter, Sian returned to her seat, her face a tight mask of control. Sharon smiled at her with sympathy.

'So, what's it like working for the man himself?'

Sian pulled a face. 'Ask me a month from now.'

'That bad?'

'Well, he's not Mr Wheatley, that's for sure.'

Sharon laughed. 'I should think not. Old Wheatley is a pussycat. Blair Davenport is a full-grown tiger. He should liven you up a bit.'

Sian looked at her in surprise. 'Do you think I need livening up?'

'No,' Sharon grinned, 'but I don't think you're going to have much choice. He's quite dynamic. If I didn't have David... Well, I might have chanced my arm.'

'Don't even imagine it, Sharon. Stick to David where you're well off,' Sian retorted shortly.

That had her friend sobering rapidly. 'What is your type of man, Sian? It can't really be Ralph. He's so...safe.'

Sian couldn't stop herself flushing. 'We can't all like macho men,' she pointed out.

'True, but you don't seem keen on men at all. Don't you want to fall in love?'

Sian felt the muscles of her face tighten up. 'I've been there, Sharon, and believe me, I've no intention of getting involved again.'

At once Sharon was full of remorse, reaching out to cover Sian's hand with her own. 'You were hurt? I'm sorry. I shouldn't have mentioned it.'

'That's OK. Besides, it wasn't the way you mean.'

Sharon groaned. 'Oh, lord, I wish you hadn't said that. Now I'm more curious than I was before.'

Getting to her feet, Sian gathered up her purse. 'Maybe I'll tell you all about it one day.' When it didn't hurt so much. 'I'm going to freshen up. I won't be long.'

In the cloakroom, Sian splashed her cheeks with cold water and paused for breath, studying her reflection in the full-length mirror. Sharon was right about the way she distanced herself from men. When you'd single-handedly destroyed someone, you didn't rush to do the same thing again. No use in saying she hadn't known how Neal would react; the truth was that her actions had precipitated him along that course. It was an awesome power she possessed, and it scared her. How could she be certain not to do the same thing again? Only by keeping herself aloof, never encouraging anyone to place their happiness on her shoulders.

Shivering, she dragged her thoughts back from those unhappy paths. Critically she turned this way and that, to view the effect of her pink crêpe dress with its long, narrow sleeves and cowl neckline. It did more than hint at her curves, it outlined them, and the back slit in the skirt allowed a tantalising glimpse of her long, slender legs.

However good she looked, she didn't feel like it on the inside. There were currents working in the air about her which hinted at things she couldn't yet see or prepare for. Like a soldier who knows he won't be returning from this battle, she sensed her own future was bound on a course over which she had no control.

Make-up repaired, Sian left the room and very nearly cannoned straight into Blair.

'Good evening, Sian,' he greeted smoothly as he steadied her, and nodded to a highly interested group of staff who happened to be walking past.

'Good evening,' she responded politely, aware they were still within earshot.

Blair ran his eye over the attractive picture she made. 'Beautiful. It's a shame it goes no further than the surface.'

'How would you know? You've never attempted to look,' Sian was stung into replying.

'I don't need to probe to know if something is rotten to the core,' Blair riposted with rapierlike sharpness. 'So, are you enjoying yourself?'

'Very much,' she responded sweetly, though her nerves had been badly rattled by his words. 'And you?'

Blue eyes gleamed. 'I always enjoy myself, although I must admit there's an added piquancy to this occasion. You've heard, I suppose, that you and I are deemed to be engaged in a torrid affair?'

Against her will she flushed. 'Yes. Are you going to scotch the rumour?'

Casually he tucked his hands in his trouser pockets and rocked back on his heels. 'My inclination is to add fire to the smoke.'

It was, after all, no more than she would have expected. 'No, Blair,' she refused flatly.

He was enjoying himself hugely. 'No to what?'

She ground her teeth. 'Whatever you're suggesting.'

His smile was sardonic. 'You haven't been asked yet.'

'Why do I get the feeling you don't intend to ask?' she countered hardily, refusing to be upset.

'Could it be because you're learning?' he asked, oh, so sweetly.

She paled, but kept her head. 'The answer is still no,' she reiterated, moving away.

To her turned back he said softly, 'You know, you really shouldn't have run. You can't expect the same kindness now.'

He wasn't pulling any punches. Eyes huge in an ashen face, Sian turned back. 'What can I expect—humiliation?'

His gaze narrowed. 'It's how Neal felt. You crucified him,' he ground out savagely.

Sian had to work her throat madly in order to speak. 'Sometimes you have to be cruel to be kind,' she said hoarsely.

His hand shot out and caught hold of her arm, dragging her close to snarl, 'You call that kindness? I can think of another word for it.'

She pulled away, her heart beating sickeningly fast. 'I'm sure you can. However, my friends are waiting for me, so if you'll excuse me...'

Without waiting for a reply, she turned and walked away, aware of his eyes on her back until, thankfully, the crowd closed around her. She was almost visibly shaking. His assurance was frightening. She wanted to run, but had vowed not to. If only there was some way she could make him understand that she hadn't wanted to hurt Neal. But if she was in his place, she would see any attempt at explanation as an excuse, a means of wriggling out of the situation. Why should he believe her? She had no proof of her father's intent. She had done her job too well all those years ago.

She had barely returned to her seat when a blood-curdling whine from the loudspeaker system drew everyone's attention to the top of the room where Tom Maynard, one of the younger directors, had taken over the microphone. By his side stood Blair, smiling broadly, laughing at something someone had just shouted to him.

'Can I have just a moment of your time, ladies and gentlemen? Ladies, especially.' Tom smiled at those nearest to him. 'Now, this isn't going to be a speech.' Howls of disbelief followed. 'More in the nature of a surprise package. Ladies, there can't be one of you who doesn't know it's leap year. It seemed to us,' he indicated Blair and himself, 'this Valentine's Day was too good an opportunity to miss. Romance is in the air. It's a night made for love. Wouldn't one of you like to come up here and pop the question to the man of your choice, and put the poor guy out of his misery?'

There was a roar of approval from the males present, but Blair had taken over the microphone and was waving them down.

'Just to show we understand how nervous you might be at the thought of rejection, I'm prepared to spice the pot by throwing in a Caribbean honeymoon to anyone brave enough. Of course, they have to be successful, too.'

A great swell of sound followed as candidates were pressed to step forward, but in the end, and as laughingly expected, not a soul took up the challenge. Tom Maynard's roguish features creased up as he surveyed the dismayed shuffling from the female portion of the audience. When silence reigned, he shrugged and laughed.

'Sorry, lads, looks like we have no takers.'

From her seat down the hall, Sian heard the joking comments from a long way off. She could hear her heartbeat echoing inside her head. For at his words a startling thought had entered her head. Did she have the courage to do it? It would be a desperate gamble. Would it be enough for him? It had to be. It just had to be.

She came to her feet on shaky legs, her clear tones ringing across the room as she called out, 'I will.'

She heard the collective gasp from around her, and felt Sharon's anxious clutching of her hand. She looked down at her friend, almost as if she wasn't really seeing her at all.

'Don't worry,' she reassured her. 'I know what I'm doing.' Or do I? she asked herself, feeling icy cold with forboding.

Sharon's jaw sagged. 'But who are you going to ask?' she cried faintly to Sian's back as she walked away.

The crowd split for her as if she were Moses and they the Red Sea. She wasn't aware of them, her gaze was fixed on her quarry standing beside a now rather bemused Tom Maynard on the stage. Blair, by complete contrast, looked vastly amused when he saw who it was, but she could see the sharp assessment in his eyes and the merest flicker of surprise.

For her part, Sian's heart was thundering along at twice the speed as usual as she prepared herself. It would be bad, but she could bear it, if only he would be satisfied. She came to a halt below them, almost oblivious to the expectant hush which had fallen.

Tom Maynard gave her an encouraging smile. 'And where is the lucky man...Miss Thomas, isn't it?'

'Sian Thomas,' Blair put in helpfully, his blue eyes mocking her lifted chin. 'Did you bring him with you, or is he in hiding?'

'He's here,' Sian confirmed, the poise he had disliked now far from evident. She couldn't smile, the tension of the moment was too strong.

For an instant Blair hesitated, eyes dissecting her, then he shrugged. 'You'd better get on with it, then, and put the poor man out of his misery.'

The moment was upon them and she didn't flinch from the task. 'Very well...will you marry me, Blair?'

The stunned silence was so loud as to be deafening. Sian looked steadily into Blair's face. He knew at once the challenge she was offering. Her eyes said: you want me humiliated, so I'm offering you this. Turn me down before all these people, and for pity's sake, be done. For an instant there were emotions in his blue eyes that blazed at her; surprise—even admiration. Then they were hidden, and she watched his mouth move. It wasn't enough for him! She closed her eyes.

'What did you say?' She asked for confirmation although his words were already carved on her heart.

His broad smile was blinding. 'I said, I will.'

In a state of shock she watched as he jumped down from the stage and reached out to draw her resisting body into his arms. She only had time to register the gleam of delight in his eyes at her reaction, before his lips closed over hers. She suffered the sensual invasion of his kiss without being able to move a muscle.

When Blair lifted his head, only she could see the derisive look he gave her. All about them, cheers and clapping had broken out, interspersed with whistles and cat-calls as the rumours were confirmed. Sian wanted to run away screaming.

'Smile, darling,' she was urged in a sexy drawl. 'You've just made me the happiest man alive. You can't tell me you expected me to say no?'

He said it loud enough for those nearest to hear him quite clearly, yet the mockery in his face was for her alone. Yes, she had made him happy. Even he hadn't thought of this.

She moistened dry lips and fixed her gaze on his attractive nose, because she simply couldn't look him in the eye, and read the exultation there. 'Of course not, d-darling. I'm delighted. Absolutely delighted.'

Blair laughed throatily and turned to the man in charge of the music. 'Put on something long and slow, will you? And go easy on the lights. I have this urge to hold my fiancée close.'

Milking the situation for all it was worth, that met with general approval, and Sian felt a blush suffuse the whole of her body. She was drawn into the unrelenting arms again as the lights dimmed and a romantic ballad filled the air. To her horror, he slowly slid his hands down until they rested low on her hips, so that she was forced into contact with the whole virile length of him

'Hadn't you better put your arms around my neck...darling, or they might just begin to wonder?' his hatefully mocking voice drawled into her ear.

Her stricken gaze clashed with his as she was forced by circumstances to do as he suggested. How he loved rubbing salt into the wound!

His hands began a slow glide up and down her spine as he directed their steps away from the brighter lights into the shadows.

'Nice try, darling, but the injured party always has the choice of weapons.'

She shuddered, her fingers clenching in the fabric of his suit. With a monumental effort she stilled her clamouring nerves. She couldn't give in now. She lifted her chin until her stormy eyes clashed with his.

'I can't let you win!' she declared thickly.

To cap it all, he laughed. 'Such passion! I'm going to love making love to you.'

Outrage set her rigid. 'If you think I'm going to let you do that, you'll be waiting till hell freezes over.'

'I won't need to wait—you gave me permission when you asked me to marry you.'

'You know damn well I did nothing of the sort,' she gasped out.

His head dipped and he nuzzled the tender cord of her neck, his lips caressing her skin. 'Why are you trembling?'

'I'm not!' she denied, while admitting to herself that she was, and quite badly. Her legs were weak and she burned along every inch that came into contact with him. How could she help but be vitally aware of him this close to? It was reaction, that was all. The unavoidable response to being held by someone you knew despised you. 'If I am, it's because I've just discovered how much I detest you.'

Again that sensual laugh bombarded her. 'Neal never told me you were such a passionate creature. I wonder why?'

'Did he tell you everything?'

'Very near. That's why I know you so well,' he declared, and pulled her suffocatingly closer.

A shock-wave vibrated through her whole system, and to her dismay she felt her body respond to the blatant provocation. Her flesh seemed to melt and mould itself to the strong contours of his, and her breathing became shallow and painful.

'You don't know me at all,' she protested, making herself go rigid and deny this awareness.

'What's the matter? Am I holding you too tight?' he mocked her reaction.

'Yes,' she agreed huskily.

He laughed. 'You're far too sexy to be held at arm's length. Why don't you let yourself go? Relax.'

He was enjoying every turn of the screw. 'With you, never!' she shot back, then every nerve leapt as his hand glided from her back and began to insinuate its way between them. She came to an abrupt halt, jerking almost frantically out of his arms. 'Blair!' she ordered him to stop in a voice totally unlike her own.

But that was only playing into his hands. 'All right, darling,' he pacified. 'I know you want to be alone with me. We'll get your bag and then we'll leave.'

A muffled snigger told her exactly why he had said it, and her skittering gaze took in the fact that they were once more the centre of attention.

Solicitously his hand cupped her elbow and steered her beleaguered figure to where her friends sat huddled in frantic conversation. She collected her bag with the minimum of fuss, feeling Sharon's anxious eyes on her strained face. She said her farewells with a tight little smile on her lips, and left them in silence.

There was no reason then to put off leaving, and she was hustled into her coat and out into the sharp February air in double-quick time. The pavements and the roads were slick with ice. Only last week London had been covered in a blanket of snow, and even the grimiest streets had sparkled a brilliant white. It was the icy air that restored a little of her composure.

Meekly she allowed herself to be ushered into his car. Blair took his seat beside her, starting the engine and letting it idle so that the heater would start blowing out hot air the sooner. His powerful frame dominated the interior of the car. Stripped of the buffering dance crowd, his presence beside her was vastly more intimidating.

The silence dragged on, and Sian felt too shaken to think of anything to say to break it. Finally Blair spoke.

'As parties go, that was one of a kind. Perhaps we've started a precedent.' He actually started laughing.

Sian stared at him in disbelief. 'It's no joke!'

He turned his head and looked at her. 'Didn't Neal tell you about my sense of humour? Never mind, I think you'll get used to it in time.'

'Never.'

He stopped laughing, but the unholy amusement was still evident. 'It was a little foolish, don't you think, to propose?'

In the darkness, Sian swallowed. 'Perhaps.'

Blue eyes cold as ice-chips viewed her defiance unmoved. 'You realise we are now engaged? You've handed yourself to me on a platter, my dear.'

'Break it,' she urged caustically. 'You have no wish to be engaged to me.'

'On a personal note, no. But I'll have to think this through. You might be a fool, but I'm not. I don't throw away golden opportunities. You might do well to remember that the next time you throw out a challenge.'

'Oh, I will,' she declared fiercely, eyes burning. 'Believe me, I will.'

He grinned. 'I'm glad you have a temper. I never did like passive women.'

'Really?' she scorned. 'So long as I don't speak out of turn, I suppose?'

He reached out a hand and traced the line of her lips. 'That's where you're wrong. I'll let you say most anything—remember, sticks and stones.' His voice softened menacingly. 'But if you're very wise, you'll never, ever laugh in *my* face.'

Sian pulled away, her nerves screaming. It seemed he didn't expect an answer; he merely indicated she fasten her seat-belt while he did the same, then set the car in motion. Shivering, she obeyed his curt command for instructions, and in no time at all, despite their slow progress due to the bad conditions, they drew up outside her building.

Glancing at the now silent, brooding man beside her, Sian didn't know how to extricate herself from the car. She couldn't offer a brief 'goodnight' as if they had just passed a fairly pleasant evening. Blair saved her the trouble. He leant across her and released the lock. The door opened, letting in a blast of freezing air.

Sian looked at him and bit her lip. 'What are you going to do?'

He twisted his head round, one eyebrow raised. 'Still the same old cry? Never fear, whatever I decide, I promise you'll be the first to know. I'll think of something appropriate. It won't hurt you to stew for the weekend. It might even prove a salutary lesson.'

He didn't say goodnight, and neither did she as she removed herself from the low car with more haste than elegance. The minute she shut the door, he gunned the engine and was away. Sian found herself watching the departing tail-lights until long after they were gone.

She was sure he would do everything in his power to scotch the engagement. After all, neither of them wanted it. He had quite a reputation for going through the female population at a rate of knots, and he wouldn't want her blocking his freedom of choice. No, the engagement would not last, but what he would choose to put in its place was a mystery certain to give her very little sleep.

The cold finally drove her inside.

# CHAPTER THREE

SIAN spent the weekend going over the flat, almost giving it a spring-clean in her efforts to keep busy and not dwell on Friday night's fiasco. On Sunday she took a long walk in the park. It was useless to sit waiting by the telephone. Blair wouldn't call. Those were not his tactics.

She discovered what they were over breakfast on Monday morning. The notice fairly leapt out at her from the page of newspaper. 'Mr and Mrs Robert Davenport have pleasure in announcing...' She couldn't believe her own eyes, and read it through twice before accepting that the notice of her engagement to Blair was actually there in printer's ink.

Stunned, she let the paper drop to the table. How could he have done it? There wasn't a scrap of doubt in her mind who was responsible for the insertion of the notice. But why had he done it? It made no sense. No sense at all. Well, he wasn't going to get away with it. Tomorrow there would be quite a different notice appearing, she would make sure of that.

The minute she reached the office, Sian didn't waste a second before crossing to Blair's door. Knocking peremptorily, she stepped inside.

Blair was seated at his large desk by the window. He looked up when he heard the door, and relaxed back in his chair with a faint smile when he saw who it was.

'I expected you before this,' he said, inspecting her thoroughly as she approached the desk. 'That shade of green suits you,' he added, referring to the blouse she was wearing. 'You should wear it more often.'

Immediately her teeth were on edge. 'I only just arrived. Besides, I didn't come here...'

'To talk about clothes,' he finished for her, drily. 'You have great legs too, but I don't suppose you want to talk about them, either.'

Coming to a halt before the desk, her hands curled into fists. 'My legs are of no interest other than they get me from A to B. Only men seem to make a fetish out of it.'

His eyebrows shot up. 'Surely a man is supposed to be interested in his fiancée's body? After all, he expects to become intimately acquainted with it.'

Sian caught back a caustic rejoinder, knowing he was being deliberately provocative to divert her from her path. She wouldn't succumb to his manipulation. She wanted answers and she was going to get them.

'Why did you send in that notice and make the engagement official?'

'Ah.' He tossed the pencil he had been playing with on to the desk and linked his fingers across his chest. 'You don't like the idea?' he probed, almost surprised, which she knew was aimed to get a rise out of her.

'You know I don't,' she gritted through her teeth.

His smile was full of an unholy pleasure. 'Which is why I did it.'

Icy fingers ran down her spine. 'What?'

Blair was only too happy to elaborate. 'I tried to think of all the possible things that could in any way make you repent your actions, and it seemed to me the worst thing I could do was keep you engaged to me—at my mercy, so to speak—until I choose to let you go.'

It was, she conceded, exactly as bad a thing to contemplate as he had suspected. He would be a constant reminder. Not that she needed one. Her own conscience never let her forget.

'That's . . . that's . . .'

'Unanswerable?' he offered, one eyebrow rising mockingly.

Anger began to build in her chest. 'If you imagine for one minute that I'm going to sit still for this, you're very much mistaken.'

He spread his hands. 'Ah, but I don't. That's the charm of the whole plan. You're going to writhe and chafe and bridle against it—all to no avail. I am the spider, my dear Sian, and you flew right into my web.'

She shuddered at the analogy. 'Not everything that flies in is caught. I won't let you run my life the way...' She stopped abruptly.

Blair's face was rigid. 'The way you ran Neal's?' he finished harshly.

Sian swallowed. Not Neal. She had been going to say, as her father had. That would have led to explanations she couldn't make, not to this man. How could she admit to anyone just what kind of man her father had been?

'I didn't...' she began, only to stop once more.

He was in there with his lancet. 'What? Kill him?'

She was vulnerable once again. 'Do you think I wanted to do that? I loved Neal!' The words she had never thought to say to him were out before she could stop them.

Blair's anger filled the room. He was up out of his chair immediately, his expression so murderous that she shrank away.

'Would you care to run that by me again?' he bit out in a voice so carefully controlled that Sian knew it would take very little for the hands that were clenching and unclenching by his sides to find a purchase about her throat.

Her chest rose and fell rapidly. 'I know you don't believe me...'

'You're right,' he interrupted. 'It's just another of your tricks, but you're trying it on the wrong man, sweetheart. I know exactly how you felt about Neal, and what you just said is so disgusting, I could...' He stopped abruptly and swung away from her, holding on to his control by a thread.

Sian stared at his back. 'This won't work. I'll have to leave.'

'Set one foot outside that door and you'll regret it.'

They were facing each other again, the air about them alive with menace. Sian had never been so frightened in her life.

'If I stay working for you, will you at least retract that notice?'

His answer was unequivocal. 'No.'

She licked her lips. 'Then I must do it.'

'I don't think so,' Blair responded quietly.

Sian could feel herself trembling. 'Who gave you the right to play God?' she demanded huskily.

His blue eyes flashed with cruel humour. 'The very question I intended asking you.'

Her nerves leapt. 'You think *I* played God?'

'Didn't you?' he barked, eyes narrowing glacially.

Which attacked her own guilt at its lowest level. With a gasp she turned away, crossing to stare blankly out of the window. Every instinct said she must leave, but how far and how fast could she go to get away from him? There was no such place on this earth. He had as good as told her that. There was only one way she would ever be free of him, and that was when he was satisfied that she had suffered the same way Neal had. It would take courage to stay, but she would never be better set to withstand him than she was now.

The thought of accepting what he had planned for her made her shiver, but it was the only way. Only, he would never make her cry. Never.

Sian took a deep, steadying breath and turned to face him. 'For how long will this ... mockery ... last?'

There was a gleam of satisfaction in Blair's eyes as he regarded her. 'That, as they say, is for me to know, and you to find out.'

'I hope you find this has all been worth it at the end,' she said tiredly.

Blair tipped his head on one side, all anger dissolved. 'You know, seeing you like this, without that fine disdain, I can almost see what Neal saw in you.'

She didn't want to talk of Neal again, yet she was forced to say, 'He was envious of you, you know.'

Blair's face closed up. 'I'm well aware of the fact. Unfortunately, I could never get him to understand he didn't need to be.'

Sian swallowed. 'Poor Neal.'

He stared at her frostily. 'As you say, poor Neal.'

She licked her lips. 'What ... when ...?'

Blair understood what she couldn't quite voice. When was the ordeal to start? 'Tonight. We'll have dinner by way of celebration.'

To Sian, it sounded like the condemned's hearty meal. 'Very well. If you've nothing else to say, I'll get on with the post.'

Blair, seated at his desk once more, eyed her reflectively. 'You're a fighter. I like that. I never thought you would make such a worthy opponent.'

From the doorway she returned the look soberly. 'In my life I've had to be, but that's another battlefield in another war.' Letting herself quietly out, she didn't see him frown, nor realise that it was some little while before he returned to his papers.

Sian poured all her concentration into her work, refusing to dwell on what the immediate future held. Blair went out late in the afternoon, telling her he wouldn't be back. His last words as he left were a reminder to her not to be late for dinner.

Heeding his words, she was ready well before eight. She had taken a long, hot bath to try and relax, but knew it would be impossible. As she lay there, she had tried to recall everything Neal had ever told her about Blair. With hindsight she could see that Neal had stood in awe of his friend. Blair Davenport had been everything he wasn't. Nothing was hard to Blair. He had an agile mind and a keen wit, excelling both academically and at sports. With women, too. His prowess there had evinced the first signs of envy in Neal's voice, and he had been looking forward to showing her off to him— as if he had won first prize for once.

How would Blair have taken that? With tact and affection. She felt sure of that. For one thing was very clear from Blair himself: he *had* loved his friend like a brother. He had probably done his best to make their differences less obvious. He must have been a good friend.

At which point she had found it impossible to lie still, and had quickly climbed out of the bath and dried herself. A good friend, she knew, made a bad enemy.

Now Sian sighed and took a last look in the mirror. She had used her make-up for dramatic effect—rather like the Ancient Britons must have applied woad. She found the simile funny in a masochistic sort of way; the Romans had won hands down. The laughter faded from her sapphire eyes. Blair would be here soon and the lesson would begin.

She stood up and smoothed down her woollen dress. The colour exactly matched her eyes and its style was deceptively demure. The long sleeves and slashed neck gave no sign that there was practically no back to speak of. A chunky silver necklace with matching bracelets and ear-rings set it off magnificently. She had suffered a qualm that in dressing this way she might be inviting more than she wanted to deal with, but it was her style, her natural flair, and she wasn't going to let him panic her into covering up. Besides, she could imagine his reaction if she did anything so rash.

When Blair arrived, her stomach plummeted, but she mentally girded her loins and went to open the door. Her breath seemed to leave her in a woosh. He looked...

'Heart-stopping!'

'You took the words...' Suddenly her brain caught up with her tongue, and she stared at him, completely disconcerted. Idiot!

'Thank you,' he accepted drily.

'You're welcome,' she retorted acidly, stepping aside to allow him to enter, when what she really wanted to do was slam the door in his face. Her eyes followed him, his movements graceful and effortless. He had been poured into a black dress-suit and white silk shirt, complete with bow-tie. It looked elegant and civilised, but it didn't disguise the sleek male body underneath. Quite the opposite, in fact. To her dismay, Sian felt her mouth go dry and her hands go clammy.

Standing in the middle of her lounge, dwarfing its generous proportions, he looked about him with interest.

'Did you decorate this yourself?'

'Yes,' she said defensively. She was proud of it, her first attempt at home-making. It had taken time and money, but the satisfaction was immeasurable. Unfortunately, compared to the cold elegance of his apartment, it paled.

As if aware of how her thoughts were running, he slanted her an amused look. 'You have excellent taste. I like it.'

The unexpected compliment brought an unwanted swell of warmth. She was aware that her colour rose. 'Thank you. Can I get you something to drink?' If he had to be here, she might as well show good manners. Yet his presence here in her home was unsettling. Heaven knew, it was unwise to invite the devil in, and hadn't she done just that?

'Not for me,' he refused politely. 'Have you lived here long?'

'About a year. I shared flats before.'

'Got tired of having men living in, did you? I imagine you'd be happier being able to send them home. It would appeal to your need to control everything around you. You'll find me altogether different.'

Sian held on to her temper by a whisker. 'My flat-mates were all female,' she informed him tightly.

Mockery was alight on his face. 'For a passionate woman like you, that would be far too restricting. However, I applaud the move. I have no intention of leaving you in the small hours.' Without waiting for the retort he sensed hovering, his eyes returned to run over her. 'Are you ready?'

She swallowed the words, witnessing his enjoyment of her caution with a sinking heart. 'I just have to get my coat.' As soon as she turned, he received the full effect of the dress.

'Determined to go down with all guns blazing, I see,' he drawled with genuine humour.

Absurdly, amazingly, and in complete contrast to only seconds before, she found herself wanting to laugh with him. It made her feel quite dizzy for an instant, before she curbed her wayward thoughts ruthlessly, stiffening her spine. 'I beg your pardon?' she reproved frostily.

Blair gave an artistic shiver. 'The temperature seems to have dropped in here. Don't you feel it in that dress? Haven't you got it on the wrong way?'

She sent him a withering look. 'Of course, you're just low enough to make a remark like that.'

Unscathed, he laughed right down into her eyes. 'I've already told you you have a beautiful body. I'm anticipating seeing more of it.'

'Don't hold your breath.'

He grinned. 'I won't, but I think I can guarantee that you will.'

Sian gasped. The arrogance of the man! She knew then, in that very instant, that she didn't want him to touch her with an intent to seduce. It was a primeval warning of danger. She would survive the encounter, but not intact. It was clear as night following day. He had to be held at arm's length at all costs.

She had never felt less like food, yet without another word she collected her coat and allowed him to help her into it. If he was surprised at her subdued behaviour during the car ride, Blair said nothing, merely inserting a cassette in the player and letting the marvellous voice of Billie Holiday float gently on the air.

Sian surprised herself by rediscovering her appetite once they were actually seated in the cosy atmosphere of the restaurant. It was due, for the most part, to Blair's putting himself out to be charming. She was thankful for it, even though she knew it was because he had been greeted by friends when they walked in, and they could hardly be seen to be arguing when they had just become engaged.

Put at ease, she enjoyed his recounting of his brother's wedding. Blair was a natural raconteur. He had an endless fund of amusing stories which he related in a sexy voice that reminded her of rich, dark chocolate. While he talked she found herself watching him. He smiled with his eyes, she noticed, fascinated, when something really amused him. If he found something privately funny, only his lips twitched.

Half-way through the main course, she realised she was actually enjoying herself. She looked across at Blair's smiling face and thought he seemed to be enjoying himself, too.

That made her take a mental step backwards. Why? That was the question. He didn't like her. So why was he lavishing on her the charm he would use on a woman he actually wanted to be with? He was supposed to be teaching her a lesson on manipulating people, not... She laid down her knife and fork, staring at the congealing food on her plate. She had been fluttering like a doomed moth in the beacon of his attraction—because he had wanted her to. Way down inside her a pain lodged. It was, she now knew, the first subtle lesson.

She looked up to realise he had stopped speaking and was watching her with brows raised in mild enquiry above eyes that gleamed.

'Did Neal ever take you to dinner, or did he prefer to keep you all to himself?' he asked, obliquely declaring that she was quite right in her assumption.

Neal again. 'Don't you know? I thought he told you everything,' she retorted acidly, feeling as if she had betrayed herself because he had done it so easily.

'You didn't like that?' he enquired sharply.

Sian sighed. 'Would you believe me if I said I didn't mind? I was glad he had someone to confide in. His parents didn't seem to care.'

Blair's expression became sombre. 'Neal was a mass of insecurities because of them. It took me years to instil in him a sense of self-worth.'

Sian swallowed painfully on her own sense of guilt. 'Which I promptly destroyed.'

His face appeared carved from the bleakest stone. 'As you say, which you destroyed.'

She spread her hands helplessly. 'What can I say to you? If I say I didn't know, you'll condemn me for my ignorance, but that is the truth, Blair. I didn't know.'

There was no perceptible change in his expression. 'Which is academic, because you're dealing with me now, and I'm not vulnerable like Neal.'

'Are you saying you have no weak spots?' she scoffed, to hide the pain of her thoughts.

He looked amused. 'We all have our Achilles' heel, darling. You can look for mine while I look for yours. That seems like a fair proposition. If you've finished with that,' he indicated her plate, 'we can order dessert, or would you rather skip on to coffee?'

As he must have known she would, Sian chose the coffee. It was while they sat over the steaming cups that Blair produced the unassuming small square box from his pocket. All the muscles in her face seemed to seize up, and as he lifted the lid on the exquisite contents Sian removed her hands from the table, balling them into rejecting fists in her lap.

Ignoring the obviousness of the manoeuvre, Blair held out his hand. 'Give me your hand, Sian,' he ordered softly.

'I'm not wearing a ring, Blair,' she refused stolidly, her blue eyes flashing angrily.

He sighed, taking the exquisite diamond cluster from the velvet cushion and holding its delicate frame between his thumb and forefinger. 'Don't be tiresome. It will be expected of you.'

'Not by me.'

He stared at her thoughtfully. 'Maybe not, but a man in my position will be expected to present his fiancée with a ring worthy of her beauty and his regard,' he taunted with gentle malice.

That stung. 'If you offered me the Koh-i-noor, I wouldn't accept it. As far as I'm concerned, it would still be under false pretences,' she managed to choke out.

Blair's eyes became unreadable and he smiled to himself. 'Yet you would have accepted Neal's ring once.'

Every atom of colour drained from her face. That was really hitting below the belt. She could feel herself shaking even as she thrust her hand forward. He could hardly miss the trembling that transmitted itself to him as he slipped the ring on, and he looked at her.

'It's not very comfortable accepting something you don't want, is it?'

Sian snatched her hand back, glaring at him. 'I don't suppose it occurred to you that you could be stepping on someone else's toes,' she challenged, whipping up anger to banish pain.

Blair relaxed back in his seat, 'You've kept very quiet about him up till now if there is someone else. Do you have an angry lover in the wings?'

About to send him a stinging retort, she caught it back in time. Maybe...

'And if I do?'

'Naturally, you'd expect me to step aside?' he probed casually, tapping his fingers on the table top.

A hair's breadth from freedom, she paused to level her voice. 'A gentleman would.'

He started to laugh, shaking his head. 'You're a trier, I'll give you that. The obvious answer is that I'm no gentleman. Consider me as Nemesis, the spirit of retribution. And as such, I know you have no lover.'

Masking her disappointment, she hedged, 'You can't be sure.'

For answer, Blair stood up and came round behind her. Resting his hands on her shoulders, he bent until his lips brushed her ear.

'Sweetheart, if he existed and was any kind of a lover at all, he would be trying to make mincemeat out of me by now. So, either you go for seven-stone weaklings, or there isn't one. Far more flattering for you if I believe the latter, surely? We'll go, shall we?'

He seemed to be one step ahead of her all the time, she thought, as she allowed him to help her to her feet and followed him outside. It was but a short journey back to her flat, and when he drew the car to a halt she was conscious of an overwhelming relief that the ordeal was at last over. She was therefore dismayed to hear the engine die and to realise Blair had other ideas. She turned in her seat and looked queryingly at him.

'That's right, I'm coming in,' he confirmed, and unlocked his door.

She wanted to ask why, but didn't. It was doubtful if he would tell her, anyway. Inside her flat, she tossed her coat over a chair and made for the kitchen.

'Make yourself at home,' she invited sarcastically as he was sinking into one of her comfortable armchairs, to which he simply raised one eyebrow. 'I'll make some coffee.'

She set a tray while the coffee filtered. Her whole body vibrated with unbearable tension, and she could feel a headache coming on. Didn't he realise she had had just about enough today, what with one thing and another?

The nerves in her stomach fluttered. Of course he did, but what she wanted didn't come into it. He was paying the piper, so he called the tune. He intended to take over her life, as he believed she had taken over Neal's, leaving her as the puppet, waiting for him to pull the strings.

The soft strains of 'Moonlight Serenade' filtered into the room, bringing her to with a start. Scowling at the milk jug she was supposed to be filling, she realised Blair had discovered her stereo. It was just another thing over which she had no control. The sense of impotence lying heavy on her heart, she picked up the tray and carried it through.

Blair's figure, minus overcoat, jacket and bow-tie, was stretched out now from a corner of her settee. His long legs extended under the coffee-table and his eyes were closed. However, they soon shot open when she put the tray down sharply, unable to resist it. Blue eyes regarded her speculatively.

Lips twitching at her small victory, she avoided looking at him as she took her cup and settled herself in an armchair.

'You're too far away. Come over here beside me,' Blair advised quietly.

Looking at him, Sian wasn't fooled by the tone. It was a command. 'I'm comfortable here, thanks,' she demurred.

'Sian,' the softly menacing voice went on, 'if you don't want me to come over there and get you, you'll do as you're told.'

She could have rebelled, but she was learning caution. Prodding a rattler left you vulnerable to a sudden, darting attack. It was wiser to move, and she did so, sitting herself reluctantly beside him.

'That's better,' he taunted. 'What man, engaged to you, would want you anywhere but by his side?'

Sian didn't deign to reply to that. Blair was enjoying his power over her, but she wouldn't add to it more than she could help. Any victory he gained had to be won, not surrendered.

'Help yourself to sugar,' she invited, between sipping steadily at her coffee. She needed the caffeine to steady her nerves.

'Thanks,' he drawled drily, adding two spoonfuls. He caught her eyeing the signs of a sweet tooth and quirked an eyebrow at her. 'I thought you'd be the first to admit I need sweetening up.'

'I'll drink to that,' she agreed, then added, 'Sugar's bad for you.'

His shrug said he wasn't worried. 'I need the energy.'

Sian pulled a scornful face. 'Oh, really? At this time of night? Are you planning on a route march?'

There was the most infinitesimal pause before he responded. 'Perhaps I'm planning to chase you round the settee,' he taunted, and laughed when Sian flinched visibly.

Silence fell as he drank and, as it did, Sian became vitally aware of his presence beside her. There was a heat coming from him, especially where his thigh came into contact with hers. She could smell his cologne too, musky and very masculine, and, underlying that, a scent that was uniquely his. She had never been so aware of any man as she was of him—not even Neal. As she sat there breathing in the essence of him, the strangest sensation flooded over her. It was as if a million tiny fires had been lighted on her skin. She could feel her very fingertips start to tingle as the fine hairs rose on her skin. More revealing yet, she could feel the brush of her hardened nipples against the soft wool of her dress.

Sian heard her own soft gasp, and felt the tide of shamed heat well into her cheeks. Hastily she sat forward to put her cup down, and used the movement to shift out of contact with him. What was happening to her? Had she gone crazy all of a sudden? When one large, warm hand descended on her bare back, Sian went rigid, almost crying out aloud at the shock her nerves suffered. Coming so close upon her discovery of her own newly awakened senses, his hand burned like a brand.

Swallowing a nervous lump in her throat, she twisted to look at him. His deep blue eyes mocked her reaction as he held out his empty cup. Taking it, she set it on the tray beside hers. His hand moved as she did, but didn't lose that scalding contact.

'So warm and silky on the outside,' his voice came from behind her, 'so desirable and full of promise. It's a criminal waste there isn't the spark of human warmth inside you,' he finished cuttingly.

Wounded, Sian gasped. It wasn't true. Why else would she have carried this burden of guilt around with her for years?

'Do you ever burn, I wonder?' he carried on. 'Have any of your lovers really reached you?'

Angry now, she faced him again. 'That, you will never find out!'

She was totally unprepared for the swift movement that had him rising and encircling her with his arms, bearing her back down until she was half lying on the small settee.

'Won't I?' he taunted, and lowered his head.

She fought him, hands bunched into fists, pushing unavailingly at his broad shoulders as his lips plundered hers. He thwarted her at every turn. Teeth nipped at her lips until she gasped, and his successful manoeuvre allowed him entry. Then, instead of the pillage she had anticipated, he began to seduce. She had always known of his reputation as a lover, but she had never expected to have that experience unleashed upon her. He tantalised her with his lips and tongue, ravishing senses that had never realised a kiss could be like that.

Her strength began to peter out, hands that had thrust him away now clenching on to his shoulders as if the world had suddenly spun away, leaving her floating in space. But that was how it felt. The only certain thing in her floundering universe was the imprint of his taut body on hers and the constant ravishment of her lips.

Something kicked inside her, igniting a warmth that spread outwards to every nerve-ending. The need to respond was born. The first tentative movements were made, lips clinging, tongue-tip finding his. It was like an electric shock, but one that went on and on, feeding off itself until she was kissing him back with an abandon that would mortify her later.

When at last he lifted his head, she moaned deep in her throat.

'So,' Blair mused, his voice throaty but alive with laughter, 'there is a fire in you, after all.'

Her eyes flew open as she became aware at last of who he was and what she had done. Shame welled up inside her. She wanted to crawl away and hide. How could she have lost control like that? With Blair, of all people! She was stricken, but knew that she had to hide it from him. There was no way she could hand him the information she had just discovered.

'I think you and I will become lovers,' was his next mind-blowing statement.

Sian's heart turned over. Those moments of madness had taught her two things. Blair would be a wonderful lover—but she must never let him have that hold over her.

She was already shaking her head. 'No.'

Blair sat up, watching in amusement as she did the same, making sure there was quite a distance between them.

'We will, some time. I'll look forward to it.' His lips softened as he spoke, as if he was already tasting the pleasure.

'I'd rather die first!'

Laughing, he stood up, reaching for his coat and shrugging into it. 'I don't think so. I think you'd rather die of pleasure in my arms.' He moved to bend over her, using a finger to tip her chin up. 'Tonight has been...very interesting. Now I think I do know why Neal was so cut up. You're quite something to lose. He couldn't hope to find another lover as hot as you.'

Painful fingers closed on her heart, and something of her thoughts must have shown on her face, for Blair went quite still.

'Tell me,' he barked harshly. 'Tell me what I'm thinking isn't true.'

'I don't . . .' she quailed, faltering. 'I don't know what you mean.'

His face carried a terrible anger. 'My God, you cold-hearted little bitch! You were never lovers, were you?' Her shocked eyes revealed the truth. 'You couldn't even give him that, could you? You were just a tease, letting him sniff around you with his tongue hanging out, begging for scraps.'

Her voice was thick, unnatural. 'That's . . . that's not true.' It wasn't. The truth was that there had always seemed to be time, and they were content to wait. They couldn't possibly have known . . . Oh, Neal!

Blair let her go abruptly, as if long contact could contaminate him. 'Just one more thing for you to pay for, darling. We'll be lovers because I say so. I'm not like Neal. I don't ask, I take. Just now you wanted me, and some day soon I'll take you. You can forget all your other lovers and what they taught you. I'll give you an experience you'll never forget.' Each word was punched out, leaving her emotionally reeling. 'Don't bother to get up, I'll see myself out. Right now I've had all I can take. I'll see you tomorrow.' With that, he turned on his heel, collected his overcoat, and was gone.

The slamming of her front door made Sian flinch. Shaking, she raised a hand to press it to her lips, and her stomach lurched. Her skin smelt of his cologne, reminding her of just how close to him she had been. Hastening into her bathroom, she stripped herself of clothes and jewellery and stepped under the shower. Tears of self-disgust mingled with the spray as she removed every last trace of him.

But she couldn't wash him from her mind. Wrapped in a towel, she curled up on her bed. She was attracted to him. The terrible truth repeated itself over and over. He knew it too, but, thank God, he didn't know the significance. He thought her experienced and he had to go on believing it, because he must never, ever know that he was the only man to have affected her that way.

She had never experienced such a violent physical attraction. Not even towards Neal, and she had loved him. She hadn't known she could feel that way.

She stared at the ceiling. Why had it had to be him? Why not someone who knew nothing of her past, who treated her as a warm human being? It was terrifying to know that Blair could have this control over her. All the more reason to make sure it never happened again.

Yet what of his threat? He meant it. What a revenge—to make her give, despite herself, that which she had denied Neal. Only, of course, she hadn't. Not that he would believe her.

As to their becoming lovers—it must never happen. Bad enough if she was an experienced woman, but in her innocence it would destroy her. So she must fight this unwanted attraction, kill it if possible, and never give him the chance to put his threat into action.

It was well into the night before she began to relax at last, and eventually she exchanged the towel for a nightdress and slipped into bed. Her last thought before sleep claimed her was that she might be in his clutches, but she wasn't going to throw herself into his arms.

# CHAPTER FOUR

SIAN gave a deep sigh and reached out to answer the insistent buzz of the intercom.

'Yes?'

'Get me the Intech file, would you? And see if you can raise MacDonald now,' Blair's disembodied voice ordered brusquely.

Sian tightened her lips. He had barely spoken a civil word to her all day. Entering his office had been like voluntarily entering the lion's den. 'Yes, Blair,' she acknowledged just as briskly, refusing to be intimidated. She had called him Mr Davenport once this morning, and had had her head bitten off for her pains.

Instead of getting up, she reached into the bottom drawer for her bag and found her packet of pain-killers. She had barely slept last night, and a headache had been taking hold all day, not helped by the tension that surrounded her constantly. She kept a carafe of water on the shelf behind her, and poured herself a glass.

She had just swallowed the tablet when the telephone rang. She reached for it with another sigh.

'Mr Davenport's office.'

'Sian?' It was the receptionist. 'I've a woman on the line who wants to speak to Mr Davenport, but she won't give me her name. Perhaps you will have better luck.'

Sian grimaced. Just what she needed to round off an awful day. 'OK, put her on.' There was the usual hiatus of whistles, buzzes and static emptiness before the call was put through. 'Mr Davenport's office. Can I help you?'

'I want to speak to Blair.' The voice was peremptory, to say the least.

Sian had little trouble recognising it, though she had only heard it once. It belonged to the woman Blair called Dee. A spark of malicious humour shot through her. She knew very well that he didn't want to be disturbed, his orders had been strict enough. The woman on the telephone was angry, and it didn't take a high IQ to realise why. It would serve him right, a small revenge compared to the one he planned.

'One moment,' she said efficiently. 'I'll put you through.' One switch to hold, the other to buzz.

Blair wasn't amused at the interruption. 'Yes?' he barked.

'Call for you,' she said sweetly, and put it through before he could object.

Replacing the receiver, Sian gave a silent whistle and began counting the seconds. He might think it was MacDonald at first, but not for long. She got up and crossed to the filing cabinet, searching out the file he had asked for. She had barely sat down again when the intercom gave a furious buzz.

His 'Get in here,' cut across her acknowledgement.

She went, taking the folder with her. Blair was at his desk as he had been all day. His shirt-sleeves were rolled up, and his dark hair was in a tangle from raking fingers. The look he sent her was deadly at twenty paces.

'Try another trick like that and you won't like the result,' he warned bitingly.

'What will you do, fire me?' she scoffed back, not in the mood to kowtow.

Blair stared at her. He looked relaxed with his elbow on the chair arm and his chin on his hand, but she knew he was always at his most deadly at such times. 'Why?' he demanded.

'She asked to speak to you,' Sian replied simply, and watched his nostrils flare.

'You knew who it was?'

'She refused to give her name.' She told him the truth as far as it went.

Blair looked dangerously amused. 'All the same, you knew who it was,' he insisted.

She couldn't quite mask the gleam in her eye. 'What did she want?' That was acknowledgement enough.

His eyes became thoughtful. 'Exactly what you assumed she wanted. Dee is not pleased.'

'Did she expect to be the future Mrs Davenport? Tell her to stick around—you'll be free again sooner or later.' Sooner, if she had anything to do with it.

Blair sat up, amusement vanishing. 'Whatever my relationship with Dee, when I tell you I don't want to be interrupted, I expect my orders to be obeyed...to the letter. Is that understood?' he informed her coldly.

'Perfectly,' she replied coolly, holding out the folder she still carried. 'The Intech file.'

It was snatched from her fingers. 'Don't push it, Sian. You haven't seen me really angry yet.'

Her 'Heaven forbid!' was supposed to be under her breath, but Blair's ears were as sensitive as Sonar. He laughed abruptly, shaking his head. 'You've got guts, lady.'

'And you'd like to see them littering the floor,' she rejoined pungently.

Blair rubbed his chin pensively. 'I think we've got enough corpses between us as it is, don't you?'

Sian blanched. Dear lord, he knew a thousand ways to kill without leaving a visible scar. 'That was uncalled for,' she muttered fiercely.

He shrugged. 'A timely reminder, that was all.' He turned his attention to the matters on his desk, shuffling papers. 'By the way,' he made it sound an afterthought, but she wasn't fooled by his deviousness, 'I'll pick you up at seven tonight. It's semi-formal. A friend of mine is opening a new exhibition of his work.'

Sian's heart sank. The one thing she had been looking forward to was going home and staying there. Disappointment made her protest. 'Must we? I have a headache.'

'Take an aspirin.' The suggestion was tossed at her over his shoulder. He didn't even bother to look up.

It made her angry. 'For all you know, it could be a migraine!' she snapped waspishly.

He did glance round then. 'Is it?'

Tempted, she took a deep breath, only to release it dispiritedly. 'No,' she admitted reluctantly.

His smile was thin. 'Seven o'clock, then. And get me MacDonald, if that's not too much trouble.'

His sarcasm grated on her nerves as she left him. Yet she knew she should have known better than to argue in the first place. She sat down and picked up the telephone. Graham MacDonald, the chief engineer, was in his office this time, and she was relieved that something had at last gone right. She put him through to Blair thankfully.

By the time she got home she felt exhausted. The only good thing about the day was that Blair hadn't mentioned last night, not even in passing. She suspected his mood was a product of their last conversation, but he had been thankfully silent.

Her headache had disappeared to a dull ache behind her eyes, and a glance in the hall mirror showed they had purple shadows beneath them. She pulled a face. Well, make-up at least would mask the worst of it, thank goodness. Kicking off her shoes she padded into the kitchen, making herself tea and toast, spreading honey on the latter to give her energy. Blair hadn't said if they were eating or not, and she needed something inside her, for lunch had been taken on the run today.

She didn't have time to sit and relax, but headed for her bathroom, taking a second mug of tea with her. She looked longingly at the bath. How she wished she could simply lie back in some scented water and let all her troubles fade away. Instead, she switched on the shower, stripped, wrapped a towel about her hair to keep it dry and stepped under the warm spray. Five minutes later she stepped out again, feeling a little more alive than she had before.

Deciding what to wear wasn't easy, but in the end she decided on a lightweight jersey in a shade of peach that did interesting things to her hair and skin, without revealing an inch more than necessary of the latter. Slipping into silky underwear, Sian sat down to apply her make-up carefully. They would be under scrutiny tonight, and she didn't want anyone to suspect that all in the garden wasn't rosy. She most definitely was *not* doing any of this for him, she told her reflection silently.

She was ready with only minutes to spare. Blair was there on the dot, looking as handsome as ever in a casual grey suit and white silk shirt. Sian had never seen him quite so casual, and was alarmed to feel her heart skip in her chest. He was attractive, dangerously so. She reminded herself swiftly that he meant her nothing but harm, and made herself ignore the information her senses relayed to her brain.

The exhibition was being held in one of those small art galleries that dotted the West End. Up until the moment they walked in, Blair had barely spoken to her. He hadn't even touched her save to help her in and out of the car. That all changed. His arm went about her waist, robbing her of breath, as they stepped inside, and it stayed there, reminding anyone in doubt that she was his possession. Sian hated it, but didn't dare risk a scene—and he knew it, finding her silent resentment vastly amusing. He used endearments too, as he introduced her to his friends. Sian ground her teeth, smiled and bore it. He was a consummate actor. No one would guess he held her in complete contempt.

During a brief lull when they were temporarily on their own, Blair glanced down at her. 'Let's get something to drink,' he suggested abruptly.

Leading her aside, he took two glasses of white wine from a table and handed her one, looking her over critically. 'You might try to relax, and not look as if you're going to your own execution.'

The criticism stung, especially as she had been doing her best. She took a sip of the now warm wine. 'If you want me to look deliriously happy, let me go. But you won't do that, so you'll have to take me as I am.'

The smile he gave her for the benefit of anyone watching didn't reach his eyes. 'Keep it up, darling, you've already got me in the mood for a fight with that stunt this afternoon.'

'Blair, darling! So you came, after all.' The throaty tones issuing from behind made them both turn. 'And the old friend!' the blonde Sian had last seen at his apartment exclaimed dulcetly.

The woman was elegantly dressed this evening in a wrap-over dress of kingfisher-blue silk. She regarded Sian coolly through a pair of large tawny eyes. Sian had the feeling they could have belonged to a lioness eyeing up her kill.

'Hello, Dee.' Blair's greeting was more polite than friendly, and Sian speculated about that brief conversation they must have had earlier.

Dee was instantly contrite. 'Darling, you're not *still* angry with me, are you?'

'I don't care to have my decisions questioned,' he replied bluntly.

Sian wasn't surprised to see faint colour rise in Dee's cheeks.

'I only wanted an explanation. Is that so unreasonable?' she protested. 'After all, it was such a shock. But never let it be said that I was ungracious in defeat. Won't you introduce us properly this time?'

'Ah, yes, you did meet my fiancée briefly, didn't you?' Blair stated smoothly, drawing Sian closer with an arm about her waist again. 'Darling, this is an old friend, Deanna Ibbotson. Dee, my fiancée, Sian.'

The two women shook hands briefly. Although Deanna smiled, Sian could feel the animosity by osmosis.

'Congratulations, you're very lucky.'

For some reason, an imp of perversity made Sian smile back and say, 'I know,' as if she meant it.

It made Deanna catch her breath angrily, but she masked it successfully. 'Well, now, this calls for a toast, wouldn't you say? Blair darling, would you be a love and get me a glass? Mine appears to be empty.'

With a wry smile he moved to obey, and in the few seconds his back was turned, the gloves came off.

Deanna's eyes narrowed dangerously. 'Don't go looking at furniture just yet, darling. I don't easily give up what belongs to me, and Blair's always been mine.' Her voice had lost its charm to become a sibilant whisper.

Sian might not want Blair, but she wasn't going to let herself be walked all over. 'I rather fancy Blair belongs to no one but himself. However, you're welcome to try and get him back—if you can.'

There wasn't time for more. Blair returned with a fresh glass of wine which he handed to the blonde. His expression was quizzical, as if he suspected what had gone on and found it amusing.

Deanna raised her glass. 'To you both. I hope you'll be as happy as you deserve.'

Sian felt like shouting 'bravo' at the twist in the tail, but merely pretended to sip her wine.

'Now I must go,' Deanna declared easily. 'I expect I'll be seeing you both around town. Do remember what I said, won't you, darling?' Her parting reminder was aimed at Sian, who watched her go with a tight little smile.

'What *did* she say?' Blair queried, sounding amused.

Sian sent him a look heavy with irony. 'She warned me off.'

He laughed. 'I gather you weren't tempted to tell her she was welcome to me?'

She tutted in mock annoyance. 'Damn, why didn't I think of that?'

He laughed again, this time humorously. 'I like it when you're cautious, it shows my point is getting home.' His hand on her elbow steered her away towards the display area and a large, manic abstract.

'Do you suppose they put this picture here because of that sign?' Blair wondered drily, and Sian's eyes strayed to where his attention was fixed. Next to the bilious work was a discreet sign pointing the way to the toilets.

Sian burst into a gurgling laugh that echoed above the conversation and drew a dozen pairs of eyes, most amused, some indignant. Hastily she took a gasping breath and moved on.

'Are you going to buy anything tonight?' she was moved to ask, unable to hide her unfavourable reaction to what she could see.

'I sincerely doubt it.' Blair's rich voice was awash with undisguised distaste.

'Then why are we here?'

'A good question.' He carried on sardonically, 'The artist is an old friend of mine. We drifted apart these last few years.'

'Presumably he landed on another planet,' she added drily. If she looked at this any more she would be ill.

It was Blair's turn to laugh, calling down criticism on his own head. Ignoring it, he slipped an arm about her waist again. 'They're pretty grim, aren't they? I suggest we do a quick once round and get out of here.'

'But your friend——' she protested, even as her feet propelled her onwards.

'I think Conrad will be relieved to see us go. The sharpest daggers in our backs are his,' came Blair's amused rejoinder.

Sian put forward no further argument. Back in the car, Blair didn't immediately start the engine, but sat behind the wheel shaking his head. Finally he threw her a rueful glance.

'Think you can stomach food after that?'

Sian laughed. 'They were awful, but I believe I could eat something.'

His grin was conspiratorial as he reached for the ignition. 'Right, supper.'

She relaxed in her seat, unaccountably warmed by the unexpected harmony. After the studied coldness of the office, the atmosphere around her soothed her nerves. At least now she had discovered he had a sense of humour.

However, she wasn't quite so relaxed when, some minutes later, Blair steered the car into the underground car park of his apartment block. She had quite naturally assumed they would be eating at a restaurant. The idea of spending any time alone with him up there set her inner alarm bells ringing. Yet not for anything would she have him know just how uneasy she was. She let him usher her into his apartment and take her coat as if she hadn't a care in the world.

'Go on through. You can choose something to go on the stereo while I rustle up the food.'

Sian did as he suggested, but once the music was playing and she had toured the room she found it impossible to simply sit and wait for him to come back. If he made her nervous when he wasn't there, she might as well be with him.

Blair was standing by the cooker when she walked into the kitchen. He looked over his shoulder when he heard her heels tap on the tiles. One eyebrow shot up.

'Is there anything I can do to help?' she asked, uncomfortably aware of that look.

He shook his head and replaced the grill, with its two steaks, under the flame. 'I don't expect you to soil your pretty white hands by doing anything so mundane as cooking.'

How she kept her temper she didn't know, but mixed with the anger was acute disappointment that he could so wilfully destroy the harmony. 'I've been feeding myself for five years. You can trust me in a kitchen,' she told him frostily.

Blair bared his teeth in a cynical grin. 'Darling, I wouldn't trust you anywhere. However, if you insist on helping, you can make the salad. You'll find everything you need in the fridge.'

She pretended the lettuce was him and chopped at it viciously, until she caught him watching her, his smile saying he knew precisely what she was doing. She desisted then and changed tack. She would show him she was no mean hand in the kitchen, and that would wipe the smile from his face. She put in all the ingredients she could find, and then added her *pièce de résistance*— a salad dressing of her own devising.

When they finally sat down to eat the meal at the breakfast bar, he surprised her by complimenting her.

'Very good. Who taught you to cook? Your mother?'

It was her turn to mock. 'You know so much about me, but you don't know my mother died when I was tiny?'

'Pity,' he rejoined smartly. 'Had she lived, you might not have turned out to be such a spoilt brat. Your father would have been well advised to turn you over his knee rather than give you everything you wanted.'

The food she swallowed lay on her stomach like a lead weight. 'My father didn't believe in corporal punishment,' she told him levelly. He hadn't needed to use it. He had ruled the house with a rod of iron. His methods had been simple—to take away the things she enjoyed most if she refused to obey his commands. She had never won a fight with him, right up till the last. Even her flight had been escape, not victory.

'Was there ever anything you wanted that you didn't get?' he charged contemptuously.

Remembered anguish tore at her. Neal. She had wanted Neal. Yet how could she admit to being loved so little that her emotional welfare was disregarded? It wasn't the sort of thing she wanted known.

'I had all that money could buy.'

'There's no finer sight than the privileged class enjoying its privileges,' he derided.

Her appetite disappeared completely and she pushed the scarcely touched plate of food away. 'I'm fully aware of your opinion of me, so can we please change the subject?'

Blair eyed her set face thoughtfully. 'Does it upset you? I'm glad something gets through. There may be hope for you yet.'

'But you doubt it,' she added bitterly.

'You forget, I've seen you stand dry-eyed while they buried a man who thought you were the sun, moon and stars.'

The memory of that day made her eyes bright with suppressed tears. 'I've cried more tears for Neal than you can ever imagine,' she averred thickly.

His lip curled. 'Tears of self-pity, no doubt. It couldn't have reflected well on you, could it? Is that why you left? Or did even your doting father find that a little hard to take? I can't imagine you willingly leaving the goose with the golden egg.'

Anger dried her eyes. 'Can't you? But surely even you know all that glisters isn't gold.'

'A contradiction, surely? Just a moment ago you said you lacked for nothing,' he reminded her.

If he had really listened he would have known she hadn't said that at all. Lord, he made her feel so tired. He never gave up! 'Did I?' she queried wearily, rubbing at her temple.

Blair pushed his empty plate away. 'What's the matter? Is your headache coming back?'

Was it her imagination, or did he sound concerned? She glanced at him sceptically. 'Much you'd care if it was.'

'I'm not a complete monster, you know.'

She laughed incredulously. 'No? I'd say you were on more than nodding terms with Torquemada. In your own way you're just as ruthless. You see everything in black and white, no grey. Does it never occur to you that you could be wrong?'

'About you? I don't think so somehow.' He stood up. Despondently, Sian rose too and began to clear up. 'Leave that,' he ordered, relieving her of the plates. 'Hetty will do them in the morning. Go on through to the lounge. I'll make some coffee.'

Sian was too tired to protest. The music had stopped. She flipped the disc over and then sat down in a corner of the couch. She didn't know how long she could take this sort of thing before he broke her down. Kicking off her shoes, she curled her legs beneath her. There was no respite from him. Even sleeping, he haunted her dreams. Not that she had slept much lately.

Closing her eyes, she rubbed at her temples with her fingers. He was right, her headache *was* returning. She didn't hear Blair come into the room, but rather sensed his presence. She lifted her lids to find him watching her.

'You're too tense,' he stated infuriatingly.

'Is it any wonder? You're hardly a soothing influence,' she returned waspishly.

He gave her a speaking look and sat down beside her. 'Turn around.'

'What for?' she asked suspiciously.

He sighed elaborately. 'Just do as you're told, hmm?'

When she reluctantly did as she was ordered, he began to expertly massage her shoulders and neck. She tensed at first, automatically, but very soon his fingers were sending tingles through relaxing muscles. Her head lolled forwards, shoulders slumping as the tense pressure was slowly released. She couldn't withhold a sigh of relief.

'Better?' he queried without stopping.

Reluctant as she was to admit it, it was. 'Much,' she conceded.

With her guard relaxed and the tension eased, she only gradually became aware of the other things. Like the warmth of his fingers on her skin, trailing up beneath her hair, and the heat slowly spreading throughout her system. Her flesh began to prickle on a charge of electricity. The rhythmic movements were hypnotic, and she found herself moulding and flexing her body to experience the greatest degree of satisfaction.

Just when she began to lean back against him she didn't know, but it impinged on a cloudy mind that it was his breath that stirred against her hair, and the heat from his body that burned her. Even so, she didn't move. He was making her feel too good with every caress of his fingers. She wanted it to go on and on. She wanted him to turn her into his arms and kiss her, and...

The intoxicating motion had stopped and she felt instantly forsaken. Still caught in a hazy dream, Sian tipped her head to send him a frown that was half confused, half annoyed. One sight of his expression was enough to render her completely horror-struck. Blue eyes blazed at her, full of sardonic amusement. He was silently laughing at her surrender, and Sian felt she wanted to die. It wasn't even as if he had set out to deliberately entrap her. The situation she was in was her own invention.

With a strangled gasp she sat upright, cheeks flaming a mortified scarlet. She was only grateful that he hadn't taken advantage. Then another thought followed fast on the heels of that one. Why hadn't he? She had been totally in his control, helpless under a wave of awareness never experienced before. Another quick glance was sufficient answer. It was all part of the game. Her teeth closed with a snap. He did nothing because he chose not to. A whim, in fact, designed to keep her off balance and wondering.

Blair stretched as he stood up, straining the material of his shirt over flexed muscles. 'I don't know about you, but I'm tired,' he declared, and sent her another mocking grin. 'I could do with a good night's sleep.'

Banking down turbulent emotions, Sian agreed. The trouble was, she doubted if she would get one, not after this latest fiasco.

He took her home then. It had been years since anyone had seen her home to her door and then hadn't at least tried to kiss her, but that was precisely what Blair did. She told herself she was glad, because she didn't want him to kiss her, even if only a short time ago she had felt differently. She simply would not play the puppet to his capricious puppet-master.

Standing in her doorway, she wished him a cool goodnight.

Blair said nothing for a second, then reached out and ran his fingertip over her lips in a brief caress that made her draw her breath in sharply. 'Goodnight,' he said with a faint smile, and walked away.

Slamming the door relieved some of her feelings, but by no means all. God, he wound her up and let her go, and she did all the wrong things like clockwork. Without switching on the light, she crossed to the window in time to see his car pulling away from the kerb. She chewed at her lip and forced herself towards some self-honesty.

Whatever his motives, he was a dangerously attractive man, and she was dangerously attracted. He stirred up the melting-pot of her emotions far too easily for comfort. One moment she would be angry, the next . . . It was so confusing. But, and this was the alarming part, it was exhilarating too. She had been living in a cocoon for five years, but no longer. Sometimes she could actually feel herself enjoying fighting him—until he said something that brought back reminders of Neal.

Neal. Guilt overwhelmed her, but from a different source. She had loved Neal, but he hadn't made her feel any of this. His kisses had been warm, full of love and a gentle passion. They hadn't produced this wild stirring of the blood.

Sian was instantly annoyed with herself for the wistfulness of her thoughts. What she felt now wasn't a good, honest, clean emotion, but something dark and ugly. She didn't *want* to feel it. She didn't want to be tempted away from the integrity of her love for Neal by a flashing-eyed Svengali.

Sighing, she went to lock up. She must keep her wits about her. The man was danger with a capital D. It would be wise to remember that. He meant her harm. If he should win . . . The very thought of it made her shudder.

# CHAPTER FIVE

BLAIR had been into the office and left again by the time Sian arrived next day. There was a note on her blotter informing her he hoped to be back mid-morning, but it didn't say where he had gone or why.

Sian sighed with relief at not having to face him again so soon. Under normal circumstances it became an ordeal to walk in with her efficient pose intact. After last night she had positively dreaded seeing the knowing look on his face.

She had plenty of work to keep her busy, thank goodness, and his absence generated more when the telephone kept ringing and she had to use her initiative deciding just what she could deal with herself. Her job was about the only thing she was grateful to Blair for. Such an opportunity might have been a long time coming if it hadn't been for him.

Mid-morning came and went without Blair reappearing. Sian finished typing out a report, made a copy, and took both into his office to leave on his desk. While she was there the telephone rang again. If Blair had been present, she would have stepped into her own office to take it. As it was, she took it on his extension. When she heard the voice on the other end of the line, she very nearly dropped the receiver. It was her father. She went cold. Why on earth was he ringing Blair?

'I'm afraid Mr Davenport isn't available at the moment. Would you care to leave a message or phone again later?' Keeping her voice level and cool while she answered his request to speak to Blair was the hardest thing to do.

There was a long pause before that well-remembered voice spoke again. 'Sian?'

She found she was gripping the receiver like grim death and her heart-rate had increased rapidly. There was no way she was going to acknowledge that. 'I'm sorry, I...'

Sir Rhodri interrupted. 'Don't be a fool, girl. Do you imagine I don't recognise my own daughter's voice?'

Sian sank down on to a corner of the desk, her legs feeling weak and trembly. 'All right, so it is me. What do you want?' She couldn't be polite, not after all that had happened.

Her father chose not to notice. 'I read the notice of your engagement.'

'Did you?' She kept her voice devoid of all warmth. She wasn't interested, now or ever.

'I rang to offer my congratulations, although I had no idea you and your fiancé worked together,' he went on.

Anger started to swell inside her. How could he talk as if nothing had happened? 'Well, now you do know, and you've told me. Was there anything else?'

This time she had annoyed him. 'Where have your manners gone begging, young lady? Just remember who it is you're talking to.'

'Oh, I remember all right,' she said bitterly. 'How can I forget?'

'And just what is that supposed to mean?' he demanded in return.

Sian could feel herself shaking. 'I think you know.'

'Good God! You're not still sulking over that man! After five years, I should have imagined you'd grown up.'

Sulking! Sian wanted to say so many things, they stopped her from uttering a word. Finally she managed to swallow the lump in her throat. 'I have grown up, Father.'

'In that case, the least you could do is show it,' he recommended curtly. 'Now, listen to me. I've been in the city on business the last few days, and I go home tomorrow afternoon. I wanted to invite you and your fiancé to have lunch with me.'

He had to be joking! 'No,' she refused bluntly. 'Neither Blair nor I have the time.'

'Don't have the time for what?' Blair's voice queried from behind her, and she swung round to stare at him in startled dismay. 'Who are you talking to?'

Her heart sank. 'Nothing. No one,' she lied hastily. 'Don't worry, I'm dealing with it.'

'Really?' he drawled, relieving her numb fingers of the receiver and raising it to his ear.

Sian made to leave hurriedly as Blair introduced himself to her father, but he stopped her, his fingers closing painfully about her wrist.

'Of course, we'd be only too delighted to see you. Not at all...Sian wasn't sure if I would be back before lunch...No, I'm afraid that would be out of the question...Rather short notice, I agree...Very well, we'll leave it at that.'

As soon as the receiver went back down, Sian jerked free of his hold. 'I will not have lunch with him! You had absolutely no right to say I would.'

He watched her coldly, his blue eyes laden with disgust. 'I don't think it's ever been my misfortune to meet such a selfish bitch before. You take the prize, Sian. That's your father we're talking about.'

'I know precisely who he is, no one knows better. I'm warning you not to interfere.'

'You're not even prepared to give him an hour of your time?'

Blair's whole figure was rigid with distaste, but although she knew the impression she was making, nothing would make her agree. 'No.'

He let out a breath. 'In that case, very well.'

Sian stared at him, swallowing. This was too easy. 'What do you mean?' she asked suspiciously.

Blair had gone round his desk and flipped over some papers. He looked up at her, his face inscrutable. 'It means I've accepted your decision not to go to lunch.'

'But you'll go?' she prompted, unable to stop her unease.

He smiled grimly. 'As you've declined to be present, there's no point in continuing this discussion. If you've no work to do, I can find you some.'

Sian left reluctantly. She sat at her desk, chewing anxiously at her lip and staring pensively at the closed door. She knew Blair was more than a match for her father, but she couldn't help worrying. She didn't want him to go, to come anywhere under her father's sphere of influence. Yet what could she do?

She worried about it right up until lunch time when Blair emerged from his office.

'Changed your mind?' he enquired when he saw her watching him.

Sian shook her head, her eyes following him to the door. He had his hand on it when she stopped him.

'Blair! Don't go, please.' The words left her in a breathless rush and he looked at her in surprise.

'Afraid I might tell him things you don't want him to know?' he jeered coldly.

She ignored that. She wanted to tell him, warn him to be careful, but didn't know how far to go. 'Have you ever had dealings with my father?'

'Business, you mean? We're hardly in the same line.'

Relief was heady. 'Then…you've never crossed swords at all?'

'You know, you almost sound as if you care,' he said in amazement. 'Why are you so protective all of a sudden? What do you imagine I'm going to do to him?'

Her soft gasp went unnoticed, but all the same she was relieved he hadn't realised her concern was the other way around. It shook her too, because why should she care what happened to him? It made her next words sharper than she intended.

'Oh, go and have lunch, then!' And I hope you don't live to regret it, she added silently.

All that lunch hour, which slowly stretched to two, she sat in sick apprehension. What did her father want? What was he saying to Blair? What mischief did he intend? She almost wished she had gone, for then she would at least know. This sitting and waiting was awful.

Then Blair came back. Her heart lurched as she studied him critically. He looked all right. Neither upset or angry—just normal. He gave her one mocking glance as he swept through to his office, leaving her feeling like a sack of wet potatoes. For ten minutes she sat there, debating what to do, then the need to know won.

Seconds later she knocked on his door and went in. Blair was at his desk, apparently engrossed in a mass of print-outs and unaware of her presence. Only he obviously wasn't, from the comment he made without looking up.

'Ten minutes. What kept you so long?'

Sian clamped down on an angry retort. She needed answers, not an argument. 'How did it go?' she asked eventually, heart thumping crazily in her chest.

'How did what go?' he queried absently.

Anger exploded. 'You know! Lunch with my father.'

Blair threw down his pencil and sat back to examine her flushed face lazily. 'You could have been there,' he remarked tauntingly.

Sian took a deep breath. 'Is that all you're going to say?'

His expression become steely. 'You had a choice and you made it. You can't have things both ways. It's time you realised that, Sian.'

Her hands closed into impotent fists by her sides. 'So you aren't going to tell me?'

'No.'

'God, you're a cold bastard!'

He smiled coldly. 'Good manners prevent me from returning the compliment.'

'Manners? When did you get so nice? You've never pulled your punches before.'

'Did that smart? I'm glad.' He picked up his pencil again. 'If you've said all you had to say, I've got work to do.'

Dismissed, Sian spun on her heel, closing the door briskly behind her. Her anger fizzled out like a damp squib. Troubled thoughts pursued her to her desk. Tension and anxiety constricted her chest, a sensation she had been free of since leaving home. She didn't trust her father. He never did anything without a reason. There must be an ulterior motive, for he never gave something for nothing.

She could find no answers, though, and determinedly buried herself in work for the rest of the afternoon. At ten to six, Blair emerged from his office once more.

'Almost done?' he enquired, as if nothing personal had happened to interrupt their working day. He leaned over her as she sat at her typewriter, reading the typed page.

The sudden closeness after the studied silence made her throat close over, and she was vitally aware of him. She cleared her throat. 'Just some letters to finish,' she managed to say.

He straightened up, eyes flicking over her averted face. 'Leave them. Tomorrow will do. We've been invited out tonight. I don't want to arrive and have them think I've been working you too hard.'

Sian switched off the machine obediently, trying to bring her pulse under control. 'Them? Are they friends of yours?' She took her purse from the drawer and collected her coat.

'Something like that,' he muttered obliquely, and with that Sian had to be content.

She was a little surprised when, shortly before eight, he escorted her into one of London's top hotels. Blair left her in order to speak to the clerk at the desk. When he came back again he ushered her to the lift.

'We're to go straight up,' he said in answer to her questioning look.

She really should have guessed then, but she didn't. She was too busy thinking how good Blair looked in his dinner suit. He had worn it before, of course, but she had to admit that the cut of it draped around his lean body really set her pulse racing. She was suddenly glad they wouldn't be alone tonight, for that would be too dangerous. Her hands smoothed the satin of her dress. The sleeveless bodice clung tightly to her waist, while the skirt ballooned out around her hips, only to narrow in again above her knees. Blair had insisted she dress up, and now she was glad she had, given their surroundings.

There wasn't far to go once the lift deposited them on the right floor. Blair knocked once on the door and let them in.

Sian summoned a smile for his friends, but when the solitary figure rose from one of the comfortable armchairs, it died abruptly. She halted in shock, actually feeling the blood draining from her face. No! Blair touched her arm and she looked at him. The mocking satisfaction she saw registered in his eyes roused a bitter fury in her chest.

'How dare you?'

'Temper, temper,' he chided mildly, holding on firmly to her arm when she attempted to break away.

'Let me go. I'm not staying here.'

The look he sent her was deadly. 'You are. You're going to stay and afford your father the respect he deserves,' he informed her in a brittle undertone.

'Sian, my dear.'

Her father's voice drew her head round. He was coming towards her, a tall, distinguished man with an air of success and wealth. He was smiling, but his eyes remained the coldest grey she had ever seen. He bent to kiss her cheek.

She managed not to flinch away. 'Father.'

'So you came, after all,' he declared in satisfaction.

'I didn't know it was you, otherwise I wouldn't be here,' she responded bitterly, throwing Blair a look full of loathing.

He looked daggers. 'Darling, you're being unpardonably rude,' he remonstrated pointedly.

Sir Rhodri laughed. 'Oh, take no notice of her. She simply never got used to not having her own way.' He turned to the younger man. 'Blair, I'm delighted to meet you. Lord knows, you're taking on quite a task.'

Blair shook hands. 'I know how to handle her.'

'A strong hand. That's what I found I always needed. Let me take your coats.'

Fuming, Sian handed hers over. He hadn't used a strong hand, but an iron fist.

'What can I get you to drink? They provide everything here, and if there's anything they've forgotten, I can soon ring down for it.'

'Scotch for me,' Blair replied, handing over his overcoat. 'Sian?'

'Martini, please, dry.'

'I'll get them. Sit down, won't you? I won't be long.' Sir Rhodri bore away their coats as Blair's hand steered her to the nearest couch.

'Well?' he asked as he sat down beside her.

'You didn't have lunch with him, did you?' she demanded thickly.

He shook his head. 'I already had a meeting arranged.'

'You think you've been so clever, don't you?' she charged witheringly.

Blair shrugged. 'It got you here. Now the least you can do is be polite and keep a civil tongue in your head.'

Her father come back in bearing a tray with their drinks. 'Here we are.' He studied them both as they took their glasses, then settled himself comfortably in a chair facing them. 'Your health,' he toasted them with raised glass.

Sian stared down into her glass, turning it in her fingers, but making no attempt to drink.

'Sian, you're not drinking?' There was a slight edge to her father's voice.

She looked across at him coolly. 'What do you want?' she demanded brusquely.

He spread his hands. 'To wish you well. Is that really so hard to believe?'

'Frankly, yes,' she retorted bluntly.

Sir Rhodri laughed despairingly at Blair. 'Surely a father is entitled to celebrate his only daughter's engagement? What's so threatening about that?'

'Nothing that I can see,' Blair replied shortly. 'I'm sorry. I had no idea Sian was so lacking in manners. Perhaps it would be better if we postponed this meeting to some other time?' The look he sent her promised retribution.

'Nonsense.' Sir Rhodri dismissed the idea. 'I'm pretty certain that Sian will think better of this rather petty behaviour. In the past I had no trouble dealing with her moods, and I'm sure I can disperse them now.' He reached over to place his hand on her knee confidingly. 'After all, my dear, we don't want Blair—inconvenienced—do we?'

There was barely a pause, but she picked up the message loud and clear. Her heart seemed to constrict in her chest at the threat and she felt sick. That dreadful feeling of helplessness, which had been so much a part of her childhood, returned to assail her. However much she knew it was ridiculous to feel so intimidated at her age, she was. Her father's threats simply could not be ignored.

She licked her lips. 'No. No, of course not.'

Sir Rhodri sat back with a sigh and a smile. 'Then shall we eat?' he suggested cheerfully.

The next hour or so was dreadful. Her father seemed to take a delight in turning the conversation her way, forcing her to answer and keep the talk flowing. He

wanted to know all she had been doing these last few
years, and made it sound as if he had been hurt by her
desertion. All for Blair's benefit. Most of her meal went
untouched, but the two men ate heartily. They con-
versed easily too, finding a great deal to talk about, enjoying each other's jokes. Blair wasn't awed, he handled
the older man quite skilfully. Sian should have been impressed. Perhaps deep down she was, but she was too
angry now to know it. She hated them both violently,
and longed for the moment when she could leave. Once,
she caught Blair looking at her, finding her subdued behaviour highly amusing. No doubt he thought it served
her right to be 'told off' by her father. Impotent rage
began to simmer in her heart.

The evening dragged on interminably, but finally Blair
insisted that they had to leave. He went off to fetch their
coats, leaving her and her father together. She suspected
it was a deliberate ploy.

Sian lifted her chin. 'Don't imagine this changes anything. After tonight, I won't be seeing you again.'

Her father slipped his hands into his pockets and
smiled. 'Blair seems to be just the man to school you.
He won't take any of your nonsense.'

She refused to rise to that. 'Why did you really want
to see me?'

'I told you why. I wanted to wish you happy.'

'Don't give me that! Have you forgotten Neal?'

His lips thinned angrily. 'We won't go into that.'

'I won't let you do anything to Blair, Father.'

He sighed. 'I have no intention of doing anything to
him. I admire him. He's a man after my own heart. I
wish you well, Sian.'

Sian recognised in disbelief that he actually meant it.
'Why couldn't you have wished me well five years ago?'

'You're raking over dead ashes. You have Blair now.
Don't lose a good man out of bitterness,' Sir Rhodri
advised.

Sian stared at him incredulously. 'I *had* a good man,' she burst out angrily.

Her father's face took on a sneer. 'How long do you imagine you would have stayed married to Neal Fellowes? He was weak. You were the strong one. I didn't kill him, neither did you. He did it himself. The man had no backbone. None of that brood do. Look at him. He took to the bottle as if it was an old friend. His mother was an alcoholic and so would he have been. Face the facts, my dear, as they really are. He was so weak that you would have ended up despising him for it.'

'You seem to think that excuses what you did!'

'I'm not looking for excuses. I don't need them. I don't go in for mawkish sentiment. If I had the time over, I'd do the same thing. So would you—so would he,' he finished tellingly.

'Are you trying to say now that you saved me from making a big mistake?' she demanded with awful calm.

'I have always done what I considered to be the best for you.'

She meant to strike him, she even raised her hand, but was foiled at the last minute.

'For heaven's sake!'

It was Blair's disbelieving exclamation and his hand that clamped down heavily on her arm. She struggled for freedom and gained it. Grabbing her coat from the floor where Blair had dropped it, she ran from the room without looking back.

Blair caught her up in the corridor. His hand bit in hard on her arm as he hustled her along to the lift. It wasn't empty, so there wasn't a chance for him to say all that his explosive expression heralded. That had to wait until he had bundled her into the car.

'That was some exhibition you put on,' he declared cuttingly.

Sian huddled into her seat. 'Just leave me alone!'

'And let you get away with behaviour like that? No way.'

All the anger, bitterness and resentment overflowed, and she turned on him. 'Back off, Blair. Don't interfere in something you'll never understand!'

His brow darkened. 'I understand this. That you're a spoilt, selfish brat.'

'Words! They're just words! What can they do? You'll never get to me that way!' she jeered.

'You're darn right! There's a much better way.'

Hard hands jerked her into his arms, holding her captive. One hand slid up into her hair, fastening on a handful so that she couldn't avoid the descent of ruthless, bruising lips. She fought and denied him until her throat and neck ached, and her strength began to disappear. Blair raised his head to look down at her lying limp in his arms. She saw him smile, and then his head lowered again.

This time he kissed her with a breathless sensuality. He played with her, tantalising her with lips and tongue, until all she was aware of was his mouth on hers and the delicious pleasure it was sending down through her body. Ultimately her own lips began to cling to his, begging the teasing to stop, for him to satisfy a deeper need. It was all the encouragement Blair needed. With a grunt of satisfaction, he parted her now hungry lips and slid his tongue inside, seeking out the honeyed sweetness within.

She moaned as the erotic exploration deepened, evoking a shivering response. Her tongue flickered out to meet his and the sensation was electric. Her senses swam and she slipped her arms around him to press herself closer to the source of delight.

Then it was over, brought to a painful end as Blair thrust her firmly away from him. It seemed to take for ever to get her brain working again and to realise just what had happened. Her breathing was laboured, as if she had just run a gruelling race. And there was pain, too—of sudden abandonment. She couldn't see him, only his shadow in the darkness of the car, but his voice had a slightly ragged edge, as if he hadn't remained so very cool, either.

'That's the way to get to you, Sian. That's all I have to do. You hate yourself for responding to me. You hate yourself for liking the way I make you feel. That was some joke, talking about weak spots, because it seems that I'm yours, darling.'

'I hate you!' she breathed raggedly.

Blair reached forward to switch on the ignition with a harsh bark of laughter. 'I wouldn't have it any other way.'

The journey to her flat was torture for Sian. The truth of his words beat about inside her skull, filling her with self-disgust. The minute he brought the car to a halt, she was out of the door and rushing inside the block of flats. Only when her own front door closed behind her did she feel really safe from him.

She collapsed into a chair and sat there in the darkness. How he must be laughing. He had discovered the perfect form of revenge. But he wouldn't rush to take advantage of it—oh, no! He would savour the moment, build up to it, knowing she would love it and hate it at the same time.

What could she do?

Run? He would only follow her and find her. Deny him? How? Her brain would, yes, but it was her body that responded with a will of its own.

She moaned. What else? Tell him the truth? He wouldn't believe her. She had long ago predisposed him the other way. At last she accepted that there was no plan she could make, save to take each day as it came, giving him no opportunity to take advantage of her weakness.

Sighing, she got to her feet and went to get ready for bed. But sleep proved elusive. Lying in the darkness, her thoughts kept flying to what her father had said about

Neal. Had he been weak? Certainly she had made many of the decisions for them, but not without consulting him. Did that make him weak? Sian rubbed wearily at her hot forehead. So what if he had never argued with her, always deferred to her judgement? That didn't make him weak, did it? It just proved that he had loved her as much as she had loved him.

Terrible doubts crept in. A strong man wouldn't have taken to drink. A strong man would have been angry, not despairing. Anger would have carried him through, as it had her. If only he had been more like Blair! Blair had too much strength of character to turn to drink. If he had a thirst, it was for revenge.

She pressed her hand over her eyes. Had her father been right? Would she have come to despise Neal? Was gentleness really weakness? How long would it have been before she saw the truth and hated him for it? The thought horrified her, but she made herself face it. She *had* loved Neal, but reality would have destroyed it all too soon.

Again she found herself wishing he could have been more like Blair. Then hated herself for it, because it made her feel unfaithful to Neal's memory. She didn't like the way her thoughts kept going back to Blair. He was all the things she hated most. He made no secret of his feelings towards her, and yet here she was, wishing Neal had been more like him.

Consumed with disgust, she tossed and turned the hours away until sleep finally, and thankfully, claimed her.

She had to drag herself from the bed when the alarm went off. Knowing it was likely to be a very long and gruelling day, she forced down toast and coffee, then dressed in the first thing that came to hand, which turned out to be a corduroy dress in bottle green, with black revers and leather belt. Make-up followed, a necessity with so few hours' sleep, then she was ready to go.

When she walked into her office it was to discover Blair rifling through one of the filing cabinets, swearing freely. Brought up short by his presence, her nerves suffered a severe jolt when he looked up and saw her. For long seconds they stared at each other in silence. It was Blair who broke it.

'You're late.'

She glanced at her watch. 'It's only ten to eight,' she corrected composedly, undoing her coat. For some reason her fingers were all thumbs. It sorely tried her temper. She tossed the coat on to her desk. 'What are you looking for? And for goodness' sake, stop making such a mess. I'm the one who's got to make sense out of it again.'

Blair stood back to allow her at the drawer. 'The McPherson's folder. I've checked the Ms twice and it isn't there. So much for your claimed order!' he retorted irritably.

Sian took a deep breath, 'Have you tried the Macs? It's a separate section. So many people don't know what to do with Mac or Mc.' It only took a second to look in the right place, and then she was handing it to him with a sweet smile.

He took the folder with one hand and tipped her face to the window with the other. 'Trouble sleeping?' he asked with false concern.

'Don't worry, I'll manage to get all my work done,' she retorted sharply.'

'I'm glad to hear it. That will give you plenty of time to do mine as well.'

Sian twisted round quickly. 'What do you mean? Where will you be?'

'In Scotland,' he declared with maddening lack of information.

'Scotland?' she ejaculated in surprise.

Blair started to flip quickly through the file. 'Umhmm. There's a strike up there. I'm taking the first flight

I can. You'll have to hold the fort down here until I get back.'

Her jaw dropped. 'Me?'

He snapped the folder shut and eyed her forthrightly. 'I happen to know you're fully capable of doing it. Otherwise you wouldn't be doing the job you are.'

That was a complete surprise. 'But I thought ...' The sentence tailed off into nothing.

He quirked a mocking eyebrow at her. 'Yes? You thought what?'

She managed to shrug. 'Nothing.'

Blair's laugh mocked her. 'Don't read anything into it, sweetheart. I'm a businessman. I wouldn't suffer a fool working so closely with me, even one as beautiful as you. So, you're in charge. Reschedule where you can, and use your initiative on the rest. If anything really important happens that needs an immediate answer from me, I've left a number where I can be contacted on my desk. All right?'

Feeling as if she had been tossed in the deep end, Sian could only agree.

He left an hour later. She took time then to pour herself a cup of coffee from the pot that was keeping warm on the shelf in his office. Sipping at the warm liquid, she took stock of the long list of things to do. His confidence in her ability to cope was quite a boost to her morale. She was surprised he trusted her. Yet she should have known better. Not even for revenge would he compromise his business. With a rueful sigh, she got down to work.

Friday wasn't so bad once she got herself sorted out. Then there was the weekend for her to recuperate in. She slept like a log for the first time in ages, shopped, cleaned, and took a long walk in the park on Sunday.

The beginning of the following week was hectic. It stretched her, but she was surprised just how much she enjoyed it. Perhaps there was more of her father in her than she would care to admit. Blair didn't phone, and nothing occurred to cause her to use the emergency number.

Then, coming in from work one evening a few days later, she heard her telephone ringing and hurried up the stairs to answer it before the caller rang off.

'Hello,' she gasped, made breathless by the rush.

'Where were you? In the bath?' a smooth voice mocked.

To her consternation, her throat closed over and her legs felt so weak she had to sit down quickly. 'Oh, it's you!'

'That's not a very flattering greeting,' Blair laughed.

It was unnerving to discover that she had actually missed the sound of his voice. 'It wasn't meant to be,' she snapped in consequence.

'So, you haven't missed me?' he enquired mildly.

'No,' she told him baldly.

'Hmm, I'll have to test the accuracy of that when I get home,' he promised.

'And when will that be?' She would make a point of being out.

'I'll be flying home tomorrow night. I hoped you would be able to feed a hungry traveller.'

No way! 'There are restaurants,' she reminded him. To her surprise, he gave a rather tired sigh.

'Indeed there are, but after these hellish days of surviving on curled sandwiches and coffee, I was rather looking forward to a home-cooked meal. You wouldn't really condemn me to such impersonal treatment, would you?'

As a ploy it wasn't very subtle, yet what could she do? She was torn. She didn't want him in her flat, but he did sound tired. Her conscience won. 'Oh, very well, I'll cook you a meal,' she said ungraciously.

Blair gave no immediate sign of recognising her reluctance. 'That would be marvellous. Now all I have to hope is that these people don't renege.' He sighed. 'I suppose I'd better go, the meeting should be resuming any minute now. I'll see you tomorrow night then, and thanks for the offer of dinner,' he finished with heavy irony and rang off without waiting for a reply.

Sian found herself staring at a silent phone, and replaced the receiver carefully, a frown of dejection marring the smoothness of her brow. She regretted the invitation now, but couldn't recall it.

It wasn't comfortable to question why she went to quite some trouble cleaning her flat the next evening, and setting her small dining-table for two, while a rich beef casserole sent out stomach-rumbling aromas from the kitchen. Not knowing what time he would arrive, the meal was ideal, and it also gave her time for a long soak in the bath before dressing in dove-grey slacks and a pink angora sweater. Glancing in her mirror, she thought she had avoided looking as if she had dressed for the occasion.

The doorbell didn't ring until almost eight o'clock, and Sian, instantly nervous, wiped her hands on her trousers before going to answer it. Blair was leaning against the jamb, suitcase at his feet and overcoat tossed over his arm. He looked dog-tired. To her total disconcertion, all other emotions were submerged beneath a wave of concern.

She stood back instinctively to usher him inside. With the faintest of smiles hovering on his lips, he picked up the case and walked in. When she turned from shutting the door, case and overcoat were stacked by the wall and he was watching her, a rakish light burning in his eyes. Her nerves jolted wildly, but before she could react to the warning, he stepped up close and caught her into his arms.

Unprotected, Sian found herself swept into a stormy sea of passion where his lips and hands lashed at her. Her only clear thought was that he couldn't be tired at all. Then everything faded. He kissed her until she had no will of her own. With a groan, she succumbed to his undoubted supremacy. Her arms slid around him, all her plans quite overturned.

When he let her go with a deeply satisfied sigh, she blinked up at him, gasping for breath.

'I would say that we've just proved conclusively that you missed me after all,' he gibed, hooded eyes scanning her face.

She pushed herself away from him with an angry gasp as hot colour rushed up into her pale cheeks. 'You took me by surprise.'

He grinned drily. 'Don't kid yourself it would have been any different it I hadn't. Something smells good.'

Smoothing down hair ruffled by his hands, Sian found her own were shaking. She cleared her throat. 'I hope you like beef casserole,' she said, leading the way into the lounge. She waved a hand towards the settee. 'Why don't you sit down while I go and see if it's ready?'

She escaped without waiting to see if he had done as she suggested. In the kitchen she sagged against the sink, holding on tightly to the rim. How on earth had she let that kiss happen? Worse still, how could she have responded? She heard a sound behind her and stiffened, turning her head to see Blair standing in the doorway.

'Did you want something?' she asked unevenly, reaching for the oven gloves, wishing he hadn't found her in such a betraying stance.

His blue eyes followed her movements, faintly amused. 'I was wondering if there was any wine to go with the meal.'

'Oh! Well, yes, I think I do have some red. It will be in the cupboard beside the stereo. The glasses are there, too.' She managed to make a sensible answer, and sagged when he disappeared again.

She shouldn't have let him come here, but there was nothing she could do about it now. She just had to hope he wouldn't try to kiss her again. Or if he did, that she didn't succumb to it. She carried the dish through, placing it in the centre of the table. Blair had found the wine and poured out two glasses. Now he took his seat as Sian set about filling his plate. Having served him and put a small amount on her own plate, she sat down.

It seemed to her that the atmosphere was altogether too cosy. Such appetite as she possessed fled, and she could only pick at her plate while Blair tucked in with relish. She searched her mind for something to say.

'There isn't going to be a strike, then?' she said casually at last, looking up.

Blair was watching her in amusement, but he followed her lead. 'No, but it won't be long before they're at it again. This is delicious. You are a good cook.'

Sian pulled a face. 'So I can do something right?'

Blair reached for his glass and sipped at it, observing her over the rim. 'If your mother didn't teach you, where did you learn?'

'At university.' She smiled faintly at a memory. 'By trial and error.'

His eyebrows rose in mild surprise. 'No finishing school?'

She tightened her lips. 'I'm sorry if it spoils your idea of me as a butterfly, but there we are.'

His armour hadn't been dented one iota. 'What did you study?' he probed curiously.

'History.'

'And what was a girl with a history degree doing working as a secretary?'

'What most working girls do. Feeding herself and putting a roof over her head,' she admitted drily.

'Surely Daddy's allowance provided that?' he contended sceptically.

'It would, if I'd wanted it, but I wanted nothing from my father. I still don't.'

'Why not?'

Sian certainly didn't want to go into that. She abandoned her attempts to eat and stood up, reaching for his plate. 'There's ice-cream in the freezer if you would like some?'

Blair followed her movements cynically and shook his head. 'Not for me, I'm full.'

Sian controlled her temper with a deep breath. 'Coffee, then?'

He reached for her hand, eyes gleaming. 'Later. Why don't you sit down and talk to me?'

She subsided again reluctantly, nerves jangling at his touch.

'So, why wouldn't you accept money from your father? Does it have anything to do with why you wanted to hit him?' he probed deftly.

'You're like the Mounties,' Sian sighed in exasperation. 'You never give up. Yes, the two are connected, but that's all I'm going to say.'

'I'm surprised he hasn't disinherited you. Expunged your name from the family Bible.'

'He may have done, for all I know.' She shrugged. 'I can't say I'm particularly worried. Money is my father's god, not mine.'

'Isn't that rather a turn-around? I seem to recall one of your main reasons for ditching Neal was because he didn't have enough money to interest you.'

She bit her lip. 'Do you remember everything I said?' she asked painfully.

'More or less.'

'Sometimes, in the heat of the moment, we say things we don't really mean,' she declared heavily.

'In the heat of anger, I agree, but Neal hardly put up a fight. No, you meant them all right.'

'I meant to say them. There's a difference.'

His lip curled. 'I'm sure we all appreciate the subtlety.'

Sian pushed herself to her feet. 'This is pointless. Going over and over the facts doesn't change anything. You've got tunnel vision about what happened. You only see what you want to see. I hurt Neal and he died. You won't look beyond that,' she choked, her throat closing over with emotion.

Blair's face was shuttered. 'What more is there? We both know why you did it.'

Sian straightened her spine and tilted her chin defiantly. 'I know why I did it. Here's something else you can condemn me for. Given the same set of circumstances, I'd do it all again.'

The contempt on his face shrivelled her up inside. 'Lady, you are something else.'

Unable to withstand that look any more, she reached for the dirty dishes. 'I'll make some coffee,' she said huskily, and escaped into the kitchen.

Her shoulders slumped. Always he managed to goad her into admitting the truth, but in a way that made her defiant and unrepentant. It was purely a defence mechanism, so obvious that she was amazed he couldn't see it. Then, when he looked at her, he wasn't seeing her as she really was at all, only the image firmly imprinted on his own mind. If she could break through that, perhaps there would be a chance.

Her lips twisted cynically. Chance for what? His understanding? What an idiot she was!

She abandoned those impossible thoughts and concentrated instead on the coffee. When she carried it through, Blair had left the table and was standing across the room, studying the contents of her bookcase. They were predominantly history books, both fact and fiction, but there were novels too, and books on poetry and art.

When she set the tray down, he came to sit on the settee, bringing a book with him.

'Poetry?' He raised both eyebrows at her.

Put on the defensive, she stiffened. 'It isn't a crime,' she retorted quickly.

He smiled wryly. 'If it was, then I would be guilty, too.'

That did stun her. 'You read poetry?' she asked in disbelief as she curled up in one of the armchairs.

He shrugged. 'As you say, it's no crime.'

'It's hard to equate you as a romantic.'

'You don't see me as a bold knight errant coming to the rescue of innocent damsels?' he queried in amusement.

Sian had to smile at that. 'Not exactly. It isn't how I've ever pictured you.'

Blair looked intrigued. 'How do you see me?'

She gave it a moment's thought before saying carefully, 'In a long black cloak, topper, dark handle-bar moustache, pointing the way out into the cold, snowy night.'

'That's very illuminating. You see me as the oppressor, not the avenger,' he drawled slowly, as if she had given him food for thought. 'Now, I see you...' he paused, then a slow smile spread across his face '...as that mythical creature, half-woman, half-bird, who entices men with the sweetness of her song until nothing else exists and they die of hunger. A beautiful, red-headed siren.'

The barb found its mark with an accuracy that clawed at her heart. 'Hadn't you better be careful the same fate doesn't happen to you?' she charged bitterly.

'Oh, I don't think I'm in any danger,' he returned sardonically.

'The Greeks had a word for that sort of pride,' she warned.

Blair laughed. 'That doesn't surprise me. The Greeks had a word for everything.'

So, it seemed, did he, she thought caustically.

'Mind if I put some music on?'

She looked at him in amazement. This was novelty indeed, to have him asking her permission for anything.

'Actually,' she put forward, glancing at her watch, 'they're showing *Turandot* on the television tonight. I expected to miss it, but if you wouldn't mind, we could listen to that instead?' She half expected him to say no for the heck of it, but he didn't. He told her to go ahead, and made himself comfortable.

Sian went to switch on the set, selecting the right channel, then returned to her seat. After a while she glanced at him to see how he was enjoying it, and experienced a shock of pleasure to see him as absorbed as she was. When the interval came, she gave a sigh of contentment and glanced at him again. He was rubbing tiredly at his eyes.

'Why don't you stretch out? If you're going to sleep, it's better to have a short nap now than collapse at the wheel,' she suggested at once.

He gave her an old-fashioned look. 'Worried I might have an accident?'

Her teeth snapped together. 'I made the offer, take it or leave it.'

A yawn overtook him then and he looked at her ruefully. 'I think I'll take you up on it, after all.' Kicking off his shoes, he stretched out. He was asleep before the second half began.

Sian found her eyes had a tendency to stray in his direction now he was so vulnerable. In sleep, all the sternness left his face, leaving it almost boyish. A lock of hair had fallen down over his eyes, and she suppressed an urge to go across and smooth it back. With her luck, he would wake up at once, and she didn't fancy the idea of being caught in such a compromising position.

She returned her concentration to the screen and was soon lost in the drama that unfolded. When the final curtain came down, she had to wipe away emotional tears, still choked up inside by the pull of the music.

Blair was still sleeping. Silently she moved to switch off the set, then debated waking him. She decided to leave him a little longer while she did the washing up. He had to have been tired to have slept so long and so deeply. When she came back and stood over him half an hour later, he hadn't moved and was as deeply asleep as ever.

She eyed him ruefully. 'What am I going to do with you?' she sighed.

She already knew the answer. She was too soft for her own good, but she could see he needed the rest, and it seemed criminal to disturb him now. Collecting a thick blanket from the airing cupboard, she draped it over him carefully. He didn't stir. Turning off the light, she swiftly locked up and took herself to bed, hoping she wasn't going to regret her noble gesture.

Something was running up and down her back. Sian stirred and wriggled it away. It came back immediately and she rolled over with a grumpy sigh. That same something trailed across her stomach to her breast, stroking the sensitive peak. She sighed in pleasure and, when warm lips came down gently on hers, her lips parted eagerly, welcoming the sensual invasion of a velvety tongue. When those lips moved away she tried to cling on in vain. Her eyes opened in disappointment.

'Good morning,' Blair greeted throatily. 'Do you greet all your overnight guests like that?'

Her eyes opened wide in shock. Her hands groped for the duvet and tried to pull it up without success, for Blair was sitting on it. He grinned at her predicament. 'Get out!' she snapped, flushing as she remembered her reaction to his touch. 'Who said you could just walk in?'

Blair held up his other hand with its contents. 'Your coffee,' he jeered silkily and got up.

Sian immediately sat up too, and pulled the covers over her chest and under her arms. As she accepted the cup he held out, she realised he was now wearing only a towelling robe that revealed long, tanned legs, tanned forearms and good deal too much broad chest. Her mouth went dry and she hastily took a sip of the liquid. His hair was wet too, she noticed, and his jaw was dark with stubble. The sensual appeal had her stomach clenching on a wave of desire. He must have showered while she slept, and the thought of him in her small bathroom made her heart thump.

'Seen enough?'

The dulcet question brought painful colour to her cheeks as she realised she was staring.

'More than enough, thank you,' she told him in a squeaky voice. 'I'd like to see less, so if you wouldn't mind leaving...' She let the sentence trail away pointedly.

Blair stretched out a hand and lifted her chin with his finger. 'Sure that's what you really want?' he asked mockingly.

She stopped herself from pulling away. 'Absolutely sure,' she retorted firmly.

He didn't believe her, but he let her go with a laugh. 'Breakfast in ten minutes.'

When he had gone, Sian relaxed her death-grip on the cup and put it down. She should have turfed him out last night. How was she ever going to be able to walk in here without visualising the sexy picture he made? Fool! Well, it was too late now, the milk was spilt.

Climbing out of bed, she reached for her robe, wrapping the thick material around her. There was nothing she could do about the length of leg she revealed, but it made her very self-conscious as she padded towards the kitchen. On the way, she noticed Blair's case open on the the settee and realised where he had got the change of clothes.

A waft of bacon assailed her nose, and she turned her attention towards the kitchen. Blair was just serving up scrambled eggs to go with the bacon when she walked in.

'Eat it before it gets cold,' he ordered, setting the plates on the table and returning for toast and the coffee-pot.

Bemused, Sian sat down and automatically picked up knife and fork. Then she made no move to eat, just looked at him suspiciously. 'What's all this in aid of?'

Blair sat down and smiled at her mockingly. 'It's the least I could do after you gave me dinner, and let me sleep over.'

'I see. And what sort of a joke did you think you were playing earlier?' she asked tartly.

His eyes glinted as they ran over her. 'A pleasurable one, judging by your reaction,' he taunted.

Sian slammed the cutlery down, and would have stood up if he hadn't covered her hand with his, stopping her.

'You enjoyed it. Why pretend otherwise?'

She glared at him, chest heaving. 'Because I don't damn well want to enjoy anything you do!'

Her reaction pleased him. 'It's a little late for that, the horse has already bolted. Now stop the tantrum and eat your breakfast.'

Sian had to force the food down, tasting very little of it. He made her feel so impotent. How she wished she'd had the good sense to send him packing last night, after all. In future, she wouldn't make any more rash gestures.

Another thing. Why couldn't he have dressed before sitting down, instead of parading about her tiny flat in next to nothing? It made her supremely conscious that she wasn't wearing much, either. Neither did it help that the table was so small their knees kept nudging.

Altogether, by the time her plate was cleared, she fully expected to get either indigestion or heartburn—or both.

'Do you have a razor I could use? My electric one packed up on me.'

Sian's eyes flew to his jaw and then away again. 'There's an almost new one on the bath rack. You can use it if you want, but I don't have shaving soap,' she offered. It was an oddly intimate conversation to be having with the man who was her greatest enemy, and it sent a shiver along her nerves.

Blair rubbed at his jaw, producing a definite rasping sound. 'I'll manage.'

'Of course, you could leave it and go in for designer stubble,' she pointed out.

'More like designer sandpaper,' he confessed ruefully.

Sian couldn't help laughing. Standing up, she started to carry the plates to the sink. 'Well, if you're going to shave, go now while I wash up. I've got to shower too, you know,' she reminded him.

'I don't mind sharing,' he declared provokingly.

The images that flew through Sian's mind made her go hot all over. 'Well, I do,' she snapped, and didn't relax until he had left the room.

She felt queer and shaky as she washed the dishes. They had sounded sort of—settled. No rancour, merely teasing. Why couldn't he always be like that? The glimpses she saw of the softer side of him made her wistful. However, wishing the past wasn't there didn't make it disappear. Brief glimpses were all she was going to get.

Sian took her clothes with her into the bathroom when Blair left it, ignoring his quirking eyebrow at her modesty. She wasn't going to take the chance of him walking in on her. She showered quickly because time was getting on, but also because his aftershave was heady in the enclosed space, making it impossible for her to forget his presence in her flat.

Fifteen minutes later they were on their way to work, Blair with only two small nicks on his jaw to mark his stay at her place. In a day or two they would be gone, but Sian didn't think she would find it easy to exorcise his ghost.

When they reached the office, Blair was at once all brisk businessman.

'I've rough-drafted a report of my negotiations. I'd like you to get on with that immediately. I'll be calling a directors' meeting and I want everyone to have a copy in advance. Also, get MacDonald up here, will you?' He handed over the sheaf of papers from his briefcase and went into his own office.

That set the mood for the rest of the day. That brief, intimate interlude might never have happened. It was close to seven o'clock when Blair called it a day. Sian was too tired to do more than nod when he told her he had a business dinner to go to, so the evening was hers.

He watched her stifle a yawn. 'Do you like the sea?' he asked.

She blinked in confusion. 'Yes.'

'Good. I could do with a break. We'll drive down to the coast tomorrow. I'll pick you up at ten-thirty.'

Sian could have protested that she needed the weekend to catch up with the housework, but she didn't. She felt in need of a break too, and at least the sea was neutral. So she simply nodded again and let him drive her home.

Both sea and sky were violent and grey. Sian was glad she had put on her quilted parka, gloves, scarf and woolly hat over jeans and sweater. The wind constantly whipped up sand and spray to buffet their slow progress along the beach. Blair had chosen to wear jeans too, with his leather jacket and woolly hat. His relaxed clothes had matched his relaxed mood, and to Sian, who had opened her door to him without any real enthusiasm, he hadn't seemed formidable any more. He had smiled, too, and her spirits had lifted. All during the drive down, they had chatted like normal people for a change. She had experienced a crazy, bubbly sensation inside, and her cares seemed to just drift away.

As she had fallen into step beside him, she hadn't questioned why he should be so mellow, nor her reaction to it. Today was a gift horse that she had no intention of looking in the mouth.

Heads down, they battled the elements until they rounded a headland and found some slight relief.

Sian pulled her scarf down from her nose and mouth and grinned at him. 'Invigorating, isn't it?'

Cheeks bright red from the sand and wind, Blair watched the animation on her face. 'Lovely.'

Feeling more carefree than she had for weeks, Sian laughed. 'Breathe in that ozone. It's good for you.' She turned seawards to take in a lungful, and was slapped in the face by spray.

Coughing and spluttering, she wiped her streaming face and found Blair laughing beside her. Inside her chest, her heart flipped over. The change in him was breathtaking, and she found herself wishing he could always look like that. It was the first real laugh she had ever heard from him, and she had a sudden longing to hear more of it.

'Still think it's invigorating?' he enquired, tongue in cheek.

'Better than a dig in the ribs with a sharp stick, anyway,' she retorted humorously.

They walked on, absent-mindedly fossicking as they went. They stopped once to watch the progress of a yacht. Some soul was either incredibly brave or completely foolish. Sian couldn't decide which.

'Are you a good sailor?' she asked when it had disappeared from view, examining a length of nylon rope half buried in the sand.

'Tolerable,' Blair answered, coming over to give her a hand to pull it free, only to find there was nothing on the other end.

Disappointed, she dropped it and dusted off her hands. 'Neal hated the water; it could make him bilious just looking at it.' She could have bitten her tongue off as soon as she'd said it. Expecting the sort of cutting retort she had grown used to, she stole a glance at Blair. He was watching her intently.

'I know,' he said casually. 'I tried to get him on a boat once, but he damn near blacked my eye.'

Swallowing her amazement that a reference to Neal could pass without comment, Sian licked her lips, wincing at the salt taste. 'It must be awful to be afraid of something like the sea. I mean, you have to respect it—but to actually fear it, that's something else.'

'What are you afraid of?' he asked lightly.

You, the answer hovered on her lips. Instead she said, 'Storms. I hated thunder as a child. I can remember running downstairs whenever there was one. Mrs Huntly, our housekeeper, used to cuddle me.' She could recall the terror she felt even now, and shuddered. She remembered something else, too. 'My father thought it childish.'

'You *were* only a child,' Blair remarked reasonably, watching the emotions play over her mobile face.

She didn't hear him. She was years away, frowning darkly at the sea. 'Sometimes he would send me back upstairs. When he did that I used to pull the eiderdown off my bed and bury my head in it in the wardrobe. In the end I made myself stay up there.' She shivered back to reality. 'I never have liked storms.'

'Parents often do the wrong thing for the right reasons,' he declared, and, looking at him, Sian realised he thought she had been angling for sympathy.

Pride stiffened her spine. 'I didn't say that to make you sorry for me. Anyway,' she shrugged, 'it was a useful lesson, makes it easier to face things you don't like,' she told him. 'I don't suppose anything fazes you.'

'You'd be wrong. Snakes. Just looking at them makes me feel ill. They're slimy and horrible.'

She tried hard not to laugh. 'Snakes aren't slimy,' she protested reasonably.

'If phobias were rational, they wouldn't be phobias. Let's keep moving, shall we? It's too cold to stand still for long.'

They strolled on slowly.

'You told me your mother died when you were small. Who brought you up?' Blair asked a little later.

'Mrs Huntly. The housekeeper I told you about. But only until I was eight.'

He glanced across at her. 'What happened then?'

Sian looked away, frowning. She saw a shell and bent to pick it up. 'I went to boarding-school.'

Blair stopped, halting her too by clutching her shoulder. 'You're joking, surely?' He studied her face carefully.

She shrugged. 'No. Lots of children go, you know.'

'Not at eight!'

Sian pulled a wry face. 'More than you'd think.'

He digested that for a moment. Absently, they both started to walk again.

'Weren't you homesick?'

'Very,' she admitted, and lowered her lashes. 'But my father soon cured me of it,' she added flatly.

'How?'

'By not letting me come home for the short holidays. Believe me, it works,' she finished grimly. She looked up at him. 'You're shocked.'

'Anyone but an insensitive fool would be,' he declared, his expression forbidding.

She smiled cynically. 'Oh, my father was full of such good ideas.'

Blue eyes narrowed on her. 'Go on.'

Sian dropped the shell and stuffed her hands into her pockets, tucking her chin down. 'Well, he didn't believe in fairy-stories and things, said they made you soft. So when I was six he told me there was no such thing as Father Christmas. I was still to get the toys, but I wasn't to think there was anything magic about it. It was tough at the time, but at least I didn't grow up full of illusions. You have to hand it to him, he knew his stuff.'

There was a silence after that which lasted until they reached the end of the bay.

'Is that why you didn't want to see your father?'

A tanker had appeared on the horizon. Sian kept her eyes on it. 'No,' she admitted harshly. 'That was . . . something else. If you'd ever done business with my father, you'd know he never compromises. I forgot. I believed that, no matter how strict his rule was, it would ultimately bend for me, if he knew how really important something was to me. Did I say I had no illusions? I was wrong. I had one. Deep down, I hoped he really did love me. He didn't. If he had, he would never have done what he did. That's why I never want to see him again.'

'Your father has a lot to answer for,' Blair decided roughly.

Sian frowned up at him. Did that mean he understood? Her pulse leapt. 'What do you mean?'

Blair's hands came out to frame her face, and he studied her carefully. 'He transformed you from the child you were to the woman you are. If you've never received affection, you can't give it. Hurting people comes naturally to you, doesn't it?'

Sian felt as if he had somehow got inside her and was tearing her apart with his bare hands. How could he have so misunderstood what she had told him?

'That's an awful thing to say!' she choked out thickly.

'But true, none the less. The proof of it is in what you did to Neal.' He went unhesitatingly for the jugular.

'God, you're cruel!' she gasped, stricken.

'No worse than you, sweetheart.' Blair smiled thinly. 'Your father wanted you strong, but all you are is hard and bitter. Someone ought to demonstrate to you just what you're missing.'

Hurt and anger mixed in her chest. 'Are you appointing yourself?' she jeered.

'There's no one better equipped to deal with you. Think how edifying it would be for you to fall in love with me.'

Sian couldn't believe his audacity. 'That would never happen. Not in a million years!'

Blair's eyes danced with a dangerous light. 'Is that a challenge? You're fond of issuing them, aren't you? As fond as I am of taking you up on them.'

'Hah!'

He laughed, startling a pair of seagulls that had landed nearby. 'Don't be too confident. You're part-way there already.'

'That's a lie!' she denied, but her heart took an erratic turn.

'Bury that beautiful head in the sand if you want to, but I'm fully aware that you want me. You respond with a delicious abandon when you let yourself go. I can make you do that any time I care to,' he finished insolently.

'That isn't love!' she scorned.

'True,' he admitted, 'but it can be just as addictive. Neal wanted your love, but you refused to give it to him. Now you want me, and I could refuse. I could make you beg the way he did. That would be a salutary lesson.'

Sian's chest felt constricted as she stared up at him, appalled. 'Do you think I don't have any self-control? I'm not that desperate. I never could be.'

'Is that so? Then now's the time to prove it, sweetheart.'

She knew what he was going to do and struggled to prevent it, but she was no match for him. Strong arms caught her up against him as he brought his head down to hers. She tried to avoid descending lips by twisting her head from side to side, but he foiled that by using one hand to hold her head still.

Expecting an attack, she experienced instead a potent ravishment of the senses. There was nothing he didn't seem to know about arousing her response, and it was an indescribable torture to stop herself from returning those kisses. She knew she had to do it and she forced herself, but it was hard.

When at last Blair raised his head, she stared up at him defiantly, eyes sending out blue sparks. He gave a low chuckle in his throat that turned her stomach over, and rubbed a gentle thumb over bruised and throbbing lips.

'This time you win, but next time it won't be so easy, will it?' he taunted.

Sian swallowed a painful lump. Easy? It would be downright impossible, and the worst of it was that he knew it. He would take her right up to the point where she did beg for the release only he could give her, and then refuse it. What torment would it be then, compared to what she felt now?

It would be living hell, because she was dreadfully afraid that his hold on her went even deeper than she had suspected.

# CHAPTER SIX

'SIAN, I need your help.'

It was the Thursday following that disastrous ending to their day at the coast. All week Sian had kept a chilling distance between them, which should have made her feel more comfortable. It had failed for two reasons. Firstly, he hadn't attempted to follow up his words. Secondly, he had found her tactic vastly amusing.

Now, though, there was this, and she looked up at him as he walked pensively into her office, his expression grim. She waited for him to explain. Whatever the reason for his surprising statement, he didn't like it.

Blair crossed to the window and stared out broodingly. 'That was my mother on the phone,' he referred to the last call she had put through. 'She's been pestering me to meet you, and I couldn't put her off any longer. We've been invited home for the weekend.'

Sian's stomach lurched. 'You didn't say we'd go?' she cried, aghast.

He turned to her irritably. 'I've already said I couldn't put her off.'

'But you can't expect me to go and lie to all your family!'

'Why not? You've been lying to everyone else,' he pointed out bluntly.

That made her angry. 'You can't hurt acquaintances like you can family,' Sian protested.

Blair came over to her, looming over her with his hands planted firmly on her desk. 'They'll only be hurt if they know it's a lie. You're a good actress, sweetheart. So far you've managed to fool everybody, including your father. That's precisely what I'm banking on. I don't want my family to get even the briefest glimpse of what you're

110

really like, Sian. As far as they're concerned, we love each other. Projecting that image is all that interests me. We're going because we can't get out of it, but I expect a one-hundred-and-fifty-per-cent effort from you this weekend. They are not to be hurt by you.'

How dared he try to lump all the blame on her? 'What you mean is, you don't want them to know what you're doing. That's why you need my help,' she charged angrily.

Blair didn't deny it. 'And you don't want them to know just what sort of person you are. Our fight is between us, nobody else. This weekend we co-operate. We give them the image they expect to see. Agreed?'

The whole idea was totally abhorrent to Sian, yet what could she do? She looked down to where her hands were pressed tightly together. 'If I do agree to help you, what's in it for me?'

He laughed cynically. 'I might have known you'd try a deal. OK. You help me, and they'll never hear what you're really like from me.'

She glanced up, searching his face. 'You'll never tell them about Neal and me?'

Blair's lip curled. 'You have my word.'

She sighed deeply. 'All right, I agree.'

He straightened up. 'Don't get too confident. It's only a minor victory. The war isn't over. You can take to-morrow afternoon off. I'll pick you up at six.' With that, he turned on his heel and disappeared back into his office.

Sian thought of the weekend ahead and shivered. She hated the thought of deceiving his family. The only saving grace was that they weren't to know that this particular engagement would never end in marriage. It would appear to them to be just another casualty, as so many other failed engagements were.

She felt no happier during the long journey on Friday night. Sighing, she stared out of the window into the darkness, but there was nothing to see except her own dim reflection in the glass, and, beyond that, Blair's profile. She studied it closely, admiring its lines, its strength. Right now, she had no idea what he was thinking or feeling.

His reflection was no match for the substance, and she turned her head just enough to be able to watch him. He controlled the car with deceptive ease, so that even at speed she had great confidence in his ability. His dark hair was windswept and lay thickly on the collar of his leather jacket. When she had opened the door to him tonight, the vital picture he presented in the jacket, dark cords and royal blue sweater, had tugged at her senses. Watching him now, the gratification had in no way diminished. Visually, he would always have this effect on her. Blair oozed confidence—of his maleness and his inner strength. It attracted her enormously.

Blair changed down to overtake a lorry, and Sian's eyes dropped to his hand on the gear lever. It was a strong hand, with long fingers. She recalled clearly how it felt to have that same hand caressing her, and her mouth went dry, a melting warmth invading her bloodstream. She shivered, and Blair's head turned to shoot her a quick glance.

'Cold?'

'A little,' she lied, and watched as his finger flicked out to increase the flow of warm air from the heater.

'Better?' He slanted her another look.

She nodded assent, although it was already a little stuffy in the enclosed interior. On top of that she was quite warmly clad in cream cords, a chunky jumper and her coat. She watched as a smile tilted the corners of his mouth, and wondered if he had known all along that it wasn't cold she was suffering from, but something that attacked the depths of her with equal thoroughness. With a twist of her lips, she supposed he must have. He missed very little where she was concerned.

She was drawn out of her introspection when Blair steered the car off the road and on to a gravelled drive.

Within minutes they were drawing to a halt before a large, double-fronted building. All Sian could see as the headlights swept the frontage was ivy-covered stonework and the dim glow of light from behind curtained windows to the left of the front door. It was so unexpected that, when she stepped out of the car, she let her gaze wander upwards, but it was too dark to make out anything save a vague outline.

'Open the door for me, will you? It's not locked,' Blair said as he unloaded their cases.

Sian led the way inside, the warmth enfolding her immediately. Behind her, Blair shut the door with a well-placed foot, and as he did so, a door across the hall opened. The woman who emerged wasn't very tall and, Sian guessed, was somewhere in her late fifties. She was frowning, but as soon as she saw Blair straightening from depositing their cases, her face broke into a charming smile of welcome.

'Blair, darling,' she greeted warmly, crossing over to him with outstretched arms.

That Blair returned the affection was obvious as he bent to sweep her into his arms and kiss her cheeks. 'Mother, how are you?'

'I'm perfectly well, as always. Robert said he heard a car, but we expected you later. Not that I'm complaining, mind.' Mrs Davenport turned from kissing her son to do the same to Sian. 'I'm delighted to meet you at last, dear.'

'I hope you don't mind my descending on you like this,' Sian muttered nervily.

Mrs Davenport urged Sian out of her coat. 'Goodness, no! We're delighted. I have to tell you,' she said confidentially, 'the whole family is here tonight. Except John, who's still on his honeymoon. They all refused to go out until they'd met you. You're something of a minor miracle—the woman who finally caught Blair. But looking at you, I can tell he didn't run very fast. Now, come along into the warm.' And she proceeded to usher them ahead of her, rather like a sheepdog with an errant flock.

At first glance the lounge appeared crowded, but when Sian took a second to gather her composure, she realised that there were only four poeple in it. All eyes were upon her as she walked in, all showing varying degrees of curiosity. They were also unreservedly friendly. Nevertheless, she had the distinct sensation of butterflies in her stomach. She was grateful for Blair's reaching across and taking her hand, drawing her close to his side as he led her to where his father stood to welcome her.

'Welcome, Sian. Nancy was only saying the other day that this family needed another woman in it to redress the balance.' Robert Davenport's eyes twinkled at her as he bent to kiss her cheek.

'It's been male-dominated much too long, Dad.' Blair's sister Paula backed up the statement, grinning widely.

A snort from the couch announced her twin brother, Peter. 'With your hair-style, clothes and flat chest, who'd ever know you were a girl at all?'

They were as like as two peas in a pod, but despite Peter's claim there was no doubting Paula's femininity. One by one they were introduced, and Sian decided they were the handsomest-looking family she had ever seen. Including John, whose picture she was shown in his absence.

'I must say, you're brave taking on such a grouchy bear as Blair,' Paula put in as soon as they were all comfortably seated.

Conscious of Blair's arm around her shoulders as they sat on the couch, Sian cast him a look from under her lashes. 'Either that, or just too crazy to realise what I'm taking on,' she quipped. Fury began to simmer away merrily inside her. Not content with having forced her into this situation, he was leaving her to sink or swim on her own.

'Oh, Sian has her weapons, believe me,' Blair answered her attack.

'She'll need them, too.' Peter rolled his eyes expressively.

Nancy tutted. 'Now, you two, behave yourselves,' she reproved.

The twins exchanged angelic looks with their parent. 'We're always good, Mother. It's only fair that Sian should know everything about Blair before she marries him. Boy, have we got some things to tell her!'

'Stow it, you two,' Richard added his ten cents' worth and, like most elder brothers, went ignored.

Beside her, Blair appeared to be totally at ease. Sian found her own feelings were curiously mixed. She hated the thought of being here under false pretences, especially when she had received such an unconditionally warm welcome. That was the other problem. They were such a close family, yet they were welcoming her in. It was what she had always wanted, to be part of such a family. Yet, if she allowed herself to succumb to the aura of this house, she would only be hurt.

Paula leant forward from her lotus position on the floor. 'What did Blair say when he popped the question?' she weaselled cheekily. 'I mean, did he go down on one knee, or did it take place in a more intimate moment?' She juggled her lips and eyebrows suggestively.

Sian gave a choked laugh and felt the colour wash up her cheeks.

'Oh, Paula! We had enough of this the last time!' her mother remonstrated with her. 'With John's wife, Linda,' she enlightened Sian.

'Actually,' Blair spoke up, drawing all eyes, 'Sian pre-empted me. She did the proposing, didn't you, darling?' He gazed down into her shocked eyes while a buzz of surprise echoed about them.

Sian gazed at the sea of faces which studied her as if she were a strange new species, and realised Blair had dropped her in it on purpose. Everyone looked highly amused. She took a deep breath. Two, she decided, could play at this game. She spread her hands, begging their understanding.

'It's leap year,' she said. 'I made him an offer he couldn't refuse.'

Blair's eyes danced. 'I know a good deal when I hear it.' Only Sian caught the muttered, 'Touché' as he lowered his head to plant a lingering kiss on her lips.

'I think that calls for a drink,' his father declared, and rose to do the honours.

'Did you really propose, or is he just saying that?' Paula wanted to know when they all held glasses, and when Sian nodded she looked impressed. 'Wow! I wish I had the nerve to do things like that. I mean, what if he'd said no?'

While Sian almost choked on her drink at the irony of it, Blair came to her rescue.

'There was never any chance of my refusing,' he declared. He smiled, and only Sian, who met his eyes, saw the mocking message there. Nothing was forgotten, whatever impression he gave his family.

'Of course there wasn't. Now, that's enough, Paula,' Nancy ordered, in a tone Sian had heard Blair use, and her daughter subsided at once. 'Now then, Sian, I want to hear all about you. Blair tells us you now work with him.'

Sian did manage to relax a little after that. The family as a whole were charming, and before very long they were joking backwards and forwards as if she had been part of it for a long time. When she stifled a yawn behind her hand, it was Nancy who urged Blair to show her up to her room.

'I've put her at the back, dear, so she can get the benefit of the view in the morning.'

Sian smiled at her. 'I'll look forward to seeing it. Goodnight, Mrs Davenport, Mr Davenport.'

Nancy came across and kissed her cheek again. 'There's no need to be so formal, dear. You're part of the family now. You must call us Nancy and Robert, or Mum and Dad if you prefer.'

Sian's throat closed over and her cheeks grew pink. She felt the worst fraud in the world. She didn't deserve that these people should be nice to her. Blair ought to be thoroughly ashamed of himself for perpetrating such a trick!

They left the room to a chorus of goodnights. Blair retrieved her overnight case from just inside the door and joined her at the foot of the stairs. His hand at her back propelled her leaden feet upwards.

'This is awful,' she blurted out, guilt overwhelming her once more.

'Oh, I don't know. I always thought it a fair example of its type,' Blair replied equably.

Her head swivelled. 'What?'

The blue eyes were alight. 'The staircase.'

'You know darn well I didn't mean that,' she retorted in a heated undertone lest anyone should overhear them.

'God knows why, but they liked you. You seem to be able to twist just about everybody round your finger, don't you?' Blair declared easily, showing her he knew exactly what she was talking about and how she felt. He led her to the door of her room, opening it and flicking on the light. 'The bathroom is through there.' He indicated another door opposite the bed.

Sian watched him in amazement. Could he really not care how hurt his family would be when they found out the truth? 'It's not being fair to them,' she insisted.

Blair wasn't listening. He withdrew his attention from the corridor to hold out her case, his expression bland in the extreme. 'Goodnight, darling. Sleep well,' he said with a husky tremor.

Sian saw it as a deliberate goad, and her temperature rose accordingly. She took her case and his arm with it, and pulled him into the room. 'Oh, no, you don't. I want a word with you.' Her wonder at how easily he had allowed himself to be tugged inside was explained when a cheer and whistle echoed down to them from the top of the stairs. Flushing angrily, she dropped his hand as if it were red-hot.

With a laugh, Blair set her case on the bed, then casually shut the door. 'Always so impetuous, darling. You can imagine what the terrible twins are thinking now. They might even be outside, waiting for steam to come out of the keyhole.'

'Then they'll be disappointed!'

'I shouldn't count on it,' he said, advancing on her, intent written clearly on every inch of him.

Furious with him, Sian tried to evade his reaching hands, but wasn't quick enough. There was a brief scuffle, then she was locked fast against him and his lips were plundering hers. With a groan, she tried to ignore the sensuous invasion of his tongue, but it was impossible. Her lids lowered, blanking out everything but the pleasure in joining in that erotic dance. She felt the warm brush of his skin where her hands had burrowed beneath his jumper, and her fingers flexed, tracing each silky undulation.

She felt Blair shudder at her touch, heard his sudden intake of breath, and then all at once his kisses were hungry, drawing a response like molten lava. His hand found her breast and stroked it, inciting it to peak and send waves of pleasure spearing downwards, until her legs were so weak that they trembled. Then, just as suddenly, he was thrusting her from him, turning away to rake careless fingers through his hair.

'I reckon they'll be satisfied with that,' he declared ironically, facing her again, and Sian could see no trace of the passion that had swept them away only seconds ago. 'What did you want to talk to me about?'

Sian couldn't believe it. She had to use every ounce of control not to reveal her own devastation in the face if his coolness.

'I hated it, Blair. They were so happy for us,' she said unhappily.

He sighed irritably. 'Which is what we want them to be, right?' he snapped, and she could tell from his voice that he was as uncomfortable with the situation as she was. 'So if you're having second thoughts, forget it. We're in this to the bitter end. I'll see you tomorrow.'

He was gone before she could even argue. He was right though, she had no other course than to go on with what they had started, but she hated herself for it, almost as much as she hated him.

Sighing, she got ready for bed.


Nancy had told her where the stables were as they chatted over breakfast. The knowing gleam in the older woman's eyes made it impossible for Sian to go anywhere else. Her feet crunched on the gravel as she took the path through the avenue of rhododendrons. She knew it must look magnificent when they bloomed, and she felt sad that she wouldn't be here to see it. The path took a sharp left turn and she came face to face with the stable complex—an open-ended rectangle with a cobbled yard, now empty, in the middle.

Her rubber-soled boots gave no hint of her approach as she made for the building from which Blair's voice issued. The structure was old, with the spacious stalls only accessible from a passageway that stretched the entire length. Blair was so wrapped up in what he was doing that he didn't hear her come to stand in the doorway. Although the horse's ears twitched, it didn't give the game away either, so she was afforded ample time to study him.

Today he was wearing jeans and a heavy-duty plaid shirt rolled up to his elbows. She hadn't considered that his back view could be even sexier than the front, but it was. His broad shoulders tapered down to slim hips and long, beautifully shaped legs. Her eyes lingered on them the longest, her lips softening into a warm curve as her heart increased its pace.

All the while his hands moved on the glossy coat, he was crooning the sort of inconsequential nothings a mother might say to her baby. The words weren't important, it was the sound of the voice and the love it conveyed. Sian felt she could easily become envious of a horse! As she watched, Blair neatly avoided a playful bite from the magnificent creature.

The flow of affectionate invective this produced from the man made Sian's lips twitch, and when the horse bared its teeth in what she could only describe as a conspiratorial leer, laughter bubbled out of her.

Alerted to her presence, Blair's head came round slowly. 'I might have known your sympathies would be with the horse.'

Keeping her distance, Sian smiled. 'She's lovely. What's her name?'

'*He's* a gelding named Sam,' he mocked drily. 'Don't you know anything?'

Sian shrugged, then grinned. 'I know two things about a horse, and one of those is rather coarse.'

His brows went up, and he studied her in some amusement before waving her inside. 'You're in a very cheery mood this morning. Come in and be introduced,' he invited as he returned to his task.

'Sam and I will get along fine at a distance.'

His eyes threw her a challenge. 'Chicken, are you?'

'I prefer to use the word cautious.'

'Amounts to the same thing. Why were you looking for me?'

'I can leave, if you'd rather,' she told him, eyes fixed on the strong sweep of his arms and the rippling muscles of his back.

He threw her an impatient look. 'Don't be absurd.'

Rebuked, she stuck her hands in her pockets. She watched him in silence for a while. He seemed very different today, and it wasn't just the clothes. Did she have his family to thank that the coldness wasn't present in his eyes right now? He had mocked her ignorance, but it didn't have the same bite she was used to. He was relaxed, approachable, and consequently she relaxed too.

'I had a long talk with your mother over breakfast.'

'I thought you might. Mother likes nothing better than a good old-fashioned natter. She'll probably bring out all the family albums soon,' he divulged wryly.

He made her smile. 'I'll try not to laugh when we get to your baby snaps.'

Blue eyes quizzed her briefly, brows raised. 'You won't even be tempted. I was a perfect cherub, beautifully behaved. Even in my skin, and draped artistically across a cushion.'

Sian's eyes widened. 'Does she still have that one?'

Blair turned to rest his arm along Sam's back and grinned. 'I don't know, but I'd be happy to pose for you privately, to give you an idea of what it looked like.'

Sian's smile faltered, and her temperature suddenly shot through the roof as she contemplated what a picture that would be. Her cheeks went bright red.

'Not interested?' he quizzed, giving Sam a slap on the rump as he finished. He walked by her into the next stall, which was used as a store, and dropped an armful of hay over to Sam. Sian followed, almost colliding with him as he turned, dusting off his hands.

Those same hands steadied her as she reeled back a step. They didn't let her go. 'Well?'

'Maybe,' she prevaricated as her pulse galloped madly off.

His eyes, she noticed in fascination, had devilish lights in them. 'Come on, you can do better than a maybe,' he chivvied.

'Then, no.'

'Liar!'

Sian was unused to dealing with him in this mood. 'This is a silly conversation.'

Laughing, he thwarted her attempts to wriggle free. 'All you have to do, sweetheart, is tell the truth.'

'I did,' she gasped, and tried to sweep his legs out from under him in a judo throw she'd seen in the movies. She might have known Blair could do it, too.

The world tilted as her feet were swept out from under her, and she landed with a 'woosh' and a cloud of dust in the sweet-smelling hay. Following her down, he swiftly straddled her hips.

'Rat!' she croaked, swallowing and gagging on what seemed like half a ton of dust.

'Admit you lied,' Blair ordered persistently. His fingers dealt with the buttons of her coat, pushing the edges apart so that his hands could fasten about her waist.

A lump lodged in her throat. Already her heart was going crazy, and she knew if he touched her she would go up in flames.

Slowly he slipped his hands about her waist. 'If you don't want me to do what I intend to do, you'd better admit it,' he threatened.

Now her throat closed over, because part of her wanted to give him the answer he wanted, but a larger part began to dissolve in expectation of the threat. Her heart thumped wildly, but her brain made the decision and sent its signals to her voice-box. Only, she had left it too late.

Too late also, she realised she had been successfully reeled in, for he didn't start to caress her. Instead his fingers sought the sensitive area below her ribs and started to tickle.

Sian's eyes widened and she tried to scramble away. 'No! Oh, no! Don't you dare! Blair...' She was helpless in seconds as he found all the sensitive spots and tickled her unmercifully. Her heels scraped the floor as she tried uselessly to dislodge him, while she squirmed and arched this way and that to get away. Tortured laughter broke from her in gasps as she begged him to stop.

When he didn't, she doubled her efforts and very nearly unseated him. Laughing triumphantly in the face of her helplessness, he lowered himself on top of her.

Her scrabbling hands finally found a purchase in his hair. Taking a grip on two handfuls, she tugged his head up fiercely.

'Stop!' she ordered in breathless desperation.

He did, and was arrested by something he saw in her face. They stared at each other, and awareness was like an electric current shooting between them. She saw desire flare in his eyes and felt the answering heat flare up inside her. Time stopped and then started again.

They reached for each other at the same instant, her hands tightening convulsively in his hair as his arms fastened about her. With a mastery that shivered across every nerve, his lips parted hers, seeking the sweet inner sanctum with ever-deeper probes of his tongue. Sian met him half-way, feeling his muscles clench as her tongue met and matched his in an erotic dance.

Their hands reached for and found each other in caresses that bordered on the feverish. His hand sought her breast beneath her sweater, teasing her nipple into a proud, aching point that sent shuddering waves of pleasure streaking downwards. With a restless compulsion, her arm slid about him as kiss followed deep, drugging kiss.

She wanted to touch him. Beneath her fingers, his shirt was a detested barrier that obeyed her demands, pulling free of his jeans and allowing her the dizzying pleasure of splaying her hands over strong male flesh. He shuddered, but it was her too, as sensation chased sensation, desire clenching at her stomach.

With a gasp, her head fell back as, open-mouthed, he sought the frantically beating pulse at its base, his lips burning hot, his tongue a moist trail as he tasted the essence of her. She closed her eyes as his hands pushed her sweater aside. Behind closed lids, her eyes were dazzled by the electrical storm as she anticipated his touch, feeling her flesh swell and ache. Then his thumbs teased the soft underskin of her breasts as he framed her ribs, and she arched to his touch. Leaving her throat, his kiss plundered her mouth, and she responded blindly, groaning when at last his hands closed on her breasts.

Being so close was an exquisite torture, but she wanted to be closer still, and her hands fluttered down to the fastening of his jeans. It was the strength of his hand gripping her wrist that halted the movement. He lifted his mouth from hers and went completely still.

It was then Sian heard what *he* must have done—the sound of footsteps approaching. Heart knocking, she met his eyes in alarm. Blair was galvanised into action, pushing her sweater back into place, and only just in time.

'Blair? Where are you?' Paula's voice came closer. 'Mum said... oops! 'scuse me!'

Sian closed her eyes as mortified colour stained her cheeks. Being caught rolling on the stable floor had to be the worst sort of cliché. Blair, meanwhile, climbed easily to his feet and pulled her up after him. Not at all fazed, he turned to his grinning sister, tucking his shirt back into his jeans.

'Yes, Paula?' he asked with ominous calm. 'Just what did Mum say?'

Sian, peering round him as she brushed herself down, wasn't at all surprised to see Paula look extremely wary.

'Er... lunch will be on the table in half an hour,' she elucidated hastily.

'Nothing about making sure you made plenty of noise as you went, I suppose?'

Looking from one to the other of them, Sian had to bite her lips to stifle a giggle.

'Well... yes, actually,' Paula admitted. 'But I thought...' She shrugged diffidently.

'That it would be much more fun to catch us at it,' Blair finished bluntly. 'I think you owe Sian an apology for embarrassing her... again.' He forcefully reminded the younger girl of her behaviour last night.

'Sorry, Sian,' Paula apologised immediately and started to back out. 'But I think you ought to brush your hair or everyone will know...' eyes exactly like Blair's danced ' ... you've been having a roll in the hay!' she finished, and fled with a peal of laughter as her brother took an ominous step towards her.

'That girl!' he growled, but when he turned to Sian again he was smiling. That slowly faded as they stared at each other. 'Effective as a cold shower,' he drawled wryly.

Sian didn't know what to say. That was the closest she had ever come to making love, and she still felt the ache of frustration.

'Things got a little out of hand,' he added.

'It was a mistake,' she declared huskily.

He gave a bark of laughter. 'You're telling me! Wanting you is about as sensible as wanting a hole in the head. Your brand of temptation is deadly.'

'I didn't intend that to happen any more than you did!' Sian gasped, cut to the quick by his reference to Neal.

Blair shifted his weight to one leg and ran a hand through his hair. He took a ragged breath. 'No, I guess you didn't.' His fingers came away with pieces of hay. 'We'd better get cleaned up. Let me look at your hair.'

She stood patiently as his fingers combed the tumbled, fiery mass. Shivers ran up and down her spine. Now she knew why she had been envious of Sam earlier. Blair's touch was soft but sure, and incredibly sensual. Each stroke wrapped invisible fingers about her heart.

At that precise moment she knew. Standing there with Blair so very close behind her, wrapped in the aura of his personality. She had fallen in love with him.

Just when, she didn't know. She felt as if it had always been there—and perhaps it had, waiting. She closed her eyes on a wave of pain and despair she had never ex- perienced before. Not even for Neal. Then, guilt had played a hand too. Now there was the knowledge that Blair would never love the woman he believed her to be, and no matter what she did she hadn't been able to alter his opinion one iota. He was everything she had ever wanted, and must be forever out of reach.

She recalled his threat to make her fall in love with him. How he would crow if he realised that she had done it all on her own. So he must never know. Never be allowed to guess the truth. The future looked so bleak. How could she ever bear it? Not by hoping to fall out of love with him. If she had managed to fall, despite all he had ever done, then what could he possibly do to reverse it? She gasped.

'Sorry,' Blair apologised.

Sian bit back hysterical laughter. If only the worst that had befallen her was his pulling her hair!

'That's the best I can do,' he said, fluffing the mass again before turning her around. 'We'll use the side door. With any luck, we'll get to our rooms without being seen, and you can use your brush.'

She took a deep breath and smiled. 'Thanks. You're being very kind.'

Blair took her arm. 'My mother would never forgive me if I left you open to the twins' brand of humour,' he explained as they emerged from the stable into the sunlight.

Sian winced. Would everything he said hurt twice as much now? 'They don't mean any harm,' she said softly.

'No,' he agreed. 'But they'll get away with murder if they can. Actually, they're good kids. They'll tease you if they think you don't mind and can take it.'

'I don't. Besides, one weekend isn't going to strain my nerves,' she added. Which was a lie, only nothing to do with the twins. She felt him look down at her, and wondered if her voice had given her away. Apparently not.

'You're right. I was forgetting just what a formidable lady you are. Just be careful not to hurt them, OK?'

He still didn't trust her, despite her having given her word. Nothing could have pointed out more clearly just how hopeless her position was.

They entered the avenue of rhododendrons again, but all Sian felt now was the gloom closing in around her.

# CHAPTER SEVEN

SIAN was grateful the family didn't give her any time to herself. She didn't want time to think when her thoughts would be so dark. To combat depression, she flung herself into whatever was suggested. After lunch they all went out for a walk to show her the countryside could be beautiful whatever the weather or season. She enjoyed it, even with Blair's arm about her waist, keeping her constantly aware of him.

When they got back to the house the twins produced Trivial Pursuit, and they all played that until it was time to go up and change for dinner. It was to be a celebratory meal, and Margot and Simon Ibbotson, Blair's godparents, had been invited. Sian wondered what Deanna's parents would be like, but they turned out to be a very friendly couple, totally unlike their daughter.

After dinner, Richard and Peter put on some music. Everyone took to the floor and Sian found herself whisked from partner to partner. Long before the evening was over, Sian was exhausted. The strain of pretending to enjoy herself had gradually brought on a tense, nervous headache. When the Ibbotsons finally left around midnight, her sigh was one of pure relief. She didn't even have the energy to feel anxious when Blair put his arm about her waist.

'Come on, it's bed for you, sweetheart—you look done in,' he ordered firmly after taking one look at her face.

Sian wasn't about to argue with him. She wished everyone goodnight and then let him help her up the stairs. Outside her room, he paused to open the door and flick on the light.

'Will you be able to manage?'

'I'm not ill, just tired. I'll be fine. What I really need right now is to be alone.' For a moment she thought he was going to argue, which was the very last thing she needed. Instead, he stepped back.

'Very well, but if you change your mind or need anything, I'll be next door.'

Sian shut her door, wishing he hadn't reminded her of that. Her shoulders drooped. For all the good it did her, he could be light years away. Slowly she removed her make-up and changed into her nightie and robe. The bed looked inviting, but she knew she wouldn't sleep. Dimming the light down to a low glow, she made herself comfortable in the window-seat, drawing her knees up under her chin and wrapping her arms about them.

She had never felt so wretched. Neal had been a kind of agony, but nothing like this. She tried to call his face to mind, but couldn't. He was a shadowy figure now, almost entirely swamped by Blair.

Was there no hope?

Only one, and a very slim chance at that. If she told the truth, he might believe her. Then what? Come to love her? On the evidence that today he had shown a desire for her as great as her own for him? She would do better to cry for the moon! What, then? Should she just let him go? How could she do that? Deep inside her was the knowledge that this was it. If she let Blair go, there wouldn't be anyone else. Feeling that, she had to fight, didn't she? To lose that way would be better than by not even trying.

The truth was all she had.

Minutes passed, slowly turning into hours. The click of her door made her head shoot round. She had thought it was opening, but in fact it was closing. Blair trod carefully across the room to her, carrying a glass of milk. He was wearing a robe over pyjama bottoms, but no top, because she could clearly see his chest and its dark mat of hair.

His presence seemed to dominate the room, making her uneasily aware that it was late, that she was wearing very little, and that he was the most important person in the world to her. Her heart started to kick loudly against her chest.

'I saw the light and knew you couldn't sleep. I've brought you some warm milk and some aspirin.' Blair kept his voice low as he handed her the glass and produced the tablets from his pocket.

His consideration made her throat close over, and she stared down fixedly into the white liquid. 'You didn't have to go to so much trouble just for me,' she protested stiltedly.

'I'm aware of that,' he said, sitting down beside her, and she moved her toes to give him more room. 'I thought it was the least I could do to show my appreciation.'

Sian stared at him, unable to conceal her surprise. 'Your what?'

To her further surprise, he sighed. 'I know, you've a right to be sceptical. However, it is true. I appreciate the way you've been with my family. It wasn't till tonight that I saw just how much of a strain it was. You'd better drink that up before it gets cold.'

Because she didn't know what to say, it was the easiest course to swallow the tablets down with the milk. She drained the glass and handed it back. 'Thank you. I'm sorry if the light kept you awake, too. I'll probably get into bed now, so I'll be turning it off.'

Blair shrugged. 'There's no rush. I wasn't sleepy anyway. Don't worry about sleeping in tomorrow. Take as long as you like.' He stood up again. 'I'll see you in the morning.'

Sian watched him move away and thought: what am I waiting for? He was here, more kindly disposed towards her than at any other time. She should strike while the iron was hot. She swung her legs to the floor.

'Blair, don't go!' she urged in a strident whisper.

He stopped and turned at once, frowning. 'What's the matter? Are you ill?'

'No. It's just—I would like to talk to you.'

'Now? Couldn't it wait until morning?'

'Please. It's important. It's something I should have told you a long time ago.' She hastened to impress the idea on him.

Blair's eyes narrowed suspiciously. 'Confession time?'

Sian took a deep breath. 'Please?'

There was a twist to his lips as he rejoined her. 'Shall we make ourselves comfortable before we begin?'

It wasn't an auspicious start, but she tucked her legs up under her again as Blair sat down.

'I want you to know what really happened five years ago. It wasn't the way it seemed, you know,' she began jerkily.

'Go on,' he commanded without inflexion.

Sian hesitated, biting her lip before deciding she had no other option now. 'Neal was in trouble.'

'What sort of trouble?' Again there was nothing in his voice from which she could gauge his reaction.

'His business was threatened, for one thing, but it was more complicated than that. Neal had an enemy that neither of us knew about. Someone who bore a grudge against the whole Fellowes family. I'll never forget the day he came to me with an ultimatum. It was either Neal or the family. I could choose just how much or how little I hurt. At first I wouldn't believe it, but he even had a lawyer show me the information he had that could damage Neal and his family beyond recovery. I had to believe then.'

'And made your choice?'

'Yes. I put aside how much it would hurt me to give Neal up. Instead I balanced the one against the many. I *had* to give him up. If I'd chosen the other path, for selfish reasons, there was always the possibility he would find out, and then I would have lost him anyway. I thought... I *hoped* anger would get Neal through.' She took a deep, shaky sigh. 'How could I have known how it would all end?'

'Why didn't you go to your father for help?'

Blair's question was one she hadn't anticipated, and she had to think fast. 'I—I did, naturally, but he couldn't help. It was personal, you see,' she finished in some agitation. How could she ever admit that her father was the man?

Beside her, Blair moved for the first time, turning so that she could see his face. It looked harsh in the moonlight through the window. 'Assuming I accept that story, was there any need to be so bloody cruel?' he bit out harshly.

Sian flinched. 'He wouldn't give me up! What else was I to do?'

Blair was silent after that, but she could feel the tension in him, coming across at her in waves.

'Who was it?' he asked at last, inevitably.

She knew she had to make the lie convincing, and the only way to do that was to look him full in the face as she told it. 'I gave my word not to tell anyone. Neal may be gone, but the family still exist, and so does the threat.'

Blair expelled an impatient breath and raked a hand through his hair. 'Why now? Why tell me all this now?' he demanded roughly.

Sian spread her hands helplessly. 'Because I thought you were ready to listen. You never have been before.'

He surged to his feet and strode angrily across the room. 'Give me one good reason why I should believe you,' he charged.

Because I love you, she said silently. Aloud, she admitted, 'I can't. You'll either do it or not because you want to.'

He came back and tipped her face up to his in an ungentle movement. 'Do you think that because I wanted you this morning, I'm sufficiently softened up to accept anything you say as gospel?'

'No,' she choked out. 'But I can't make you believe that either, can I?'

He let her go abruptly. 'Why is it important that I do believe you?' he asked suspiciously.

Sian's colour fluctuated wildly, and her heart missed a beat. 'Firstly, because it's the truth. Secondly... secondly, because you'd hate to think you exacted revenge on an innocent person.'

Blair looked sceptical. 'I find it hard to believe you care that much for my soul.'

'I can't help that.' She sighed restlessly. 'Why is it so impossible for you to be wrong?'

He paced away again. 'That's the problem. Five years' conditioning says you're lying. Reason says it's too improbable a story to be made up. It leaks like a collander.'

She pulled a face. 'But you'd prefer it if I could give you proof?'

'Yes,' he returned bluntly.

'Then it's a question of faith, because I can't help you.' Bitterness cut her. 'In which case I'm wasting my time, because you'll never have faith in me.'

'No, but I do have faith in my own judgement. I'll think about what you've told me, but that's all. No promises.'

'I haven't asked for any.'

Blair stared at her consideringly. 'Why do you trust me all of a sudden?'

Sian met his eyes. 'I've always trusted that you meant what you said,' she told him honestly.

'I see. By natural progression, that had to be the result of what I felt. Have you considered that I could lie?' He proffered the suggestion.

'You haven't so far.'

He gave a twisted smile. 'And you put your trust in my integrity. That's a very clever move.'

She hadn't planned it that way. She had acted on the spur of the moment. Yet perhaps it had turned out for the best.

Blair flexed tired shoulders. 'I'm going back to bed. Not that I expect to sleep. Too much food for thought. I'll see you in the morning.'

'Goodnight, Blair,' she called softly as he passed through the door and shut it behind him with a soft click.

When he was gone, Sian felt the weight of tiredness bearing down on her. Wearily, she rose to her feet and crossed to switch off the light. Discarding the robe, she climbed into bed and lay staring into the darkness. She had done all she could. His 'yes' would open doors. His 'no' close them for ever. She could only wait.

Heavy lids fluttered over tired eyes. Emotionally exhausted, she slept.

None of the family remarked on the fact that she looked as if she hadn't slept. They probably put it down to the partying the night before. Blair wasn't exactly lively either, and it was only when she intercepted a look between Robert and Nancy that she finally realised his parents thought they had had words—hence the sleepless night. It was ironic that it was probably one of the rare occasions when they hadn't argued.

They left late on Sunday afternoon. Sian was sorry to go. She would miss them all. The way things were, it was supremely unlikely that she would see them again.

Blair didn't speak until they were on the motorway. When he reached out to turn off the radio, Sian's eyes flew to his stern profile. He spared her a brief glance.

'I want you to bear with me, Sian, and tell me the whole story again.'

She pulled a face. 'Are you testing me for discrepancies?'

He shot her another look. 'I did ask you to bear with me,' he reminded her gently.

Her sigh was defeated. 'I'm sorry. It's just that...' Her voice tailed off.

'You're unused to me not jumping feet-first down your throat,' he finished for her. 'I *do* understand, you know. Tell me again ... please.'

It didn't seem so easy in the cold light of day. She did her best to relate the facts she could without too much emotion. This time she was aware herself of just how implausible it sounded. When she finished, Blair only grunted in acknowledgement. She had to bite down hard on her lip to stop herself asking for his answer.

He remained silent all the way into town while Sian sat beside him, her stomach churning in anxiety. Outside her flat he switched off the engine but made no move to get out. Hands gripping the steering wheel, he stared fixedly into the darkness.

With a final sigh, he raked a hand through his hair and turned to her. 'I don't know. Maybe I'm crazy to trust you, but that story... It's too ludicrous to be true— so I have to believe it. As a rule, you're a far better liar.'

That was a backhanded compliment if ever there was one! 'Thank you,' she said wryly.

'So, OK, I'm prepared to back off.'

'You don't have to sound so pleased about it,' Sian retorted acidly, when only seconds ago she had wanted to laugh out loud with relief.

'Don't knock it,' he warned with a touch of anger.

'I'm sorry. I guess we're both a bit strained right now. It hasn't been an easy weekend,' she apologised.

'I'll agree with that,' he said ironically.

'Do you want to come in for coffee?' she offered.

Blair shook his head. 'Not tonight. I have some things to do, then I'm planning on getting an early night. I'll see you inside.'

'Don't bother.' Sian was out of the car and reaching into the back for her case. 'I'll be all right. I'll see you tomorrow.'

He didn't argue, merely reached over for the door. 'Tomorrow. Goodnight, Sian.'

'Goodnight,' she replied and went to let herself in. She didn't hear him go until the door had closed behind her.

Once inside her own flat, she dumped her things and went straight through to the kitchen to switch on the kettle. She felt curiously flat, not nearly as elated as she had expected to be. She had just got rid of an enemy, so why wasn't she jumping for joy? Because she didn't know what she had replaced him with. All too soon now, she knew she was going to find out.

Over the next two weeks she made the painful discovery that she had exchanged the old Blair for a more relaxed employer, and a fiancé who kept her firmly at a distance.

At the beginning, his friendliness had seemed like an omen of good things to come, until the first time he saw her home and gave her only the most chaste of kisses. She had had to struggle not to let her dismay show, and it had only got worse, not better.

She was so very aware of him, but to Blair she might simply have been a piece of office furniture, and hiding her feelings had become a painful necessity. Her heart ached. She knew he was only keeping up the fallacy of their engagement for a decent period, and would then give her the freedom he believed she wanted.

Only she didn't, she wanted him. She couldn't forget that in the stables that day he had wanted her too.

It was that thought that unconsciously made her pull out all the stops when she prepared herself for a party one evening. The dress she chose to wear was almost medieval. Made from the finest jersey, it had narrow sleeves that came to a point over her hands. The front lovingly followed the contours of her body, and only the sheerest underwear was possible so as not to destroy the line. From the hips, the gentle pleats of the skirt fell gracefully to her feet, while the back left her shoulder-blades and spine bare almost to the waist. It was shockingly sensual, and Sian had loved it from the moment the woman in the shop had showed it to her. She also secretly hoped it would knock Blair out. Anything was worth a try.

She left her hair loose in a flowing mass of dark red waves. It contrasted vividly with the blue of the dress which almost exactly matched her eyes. She knew she looked good. The test was when Blair arrived. Did she imagine it, or was there a spark of fire in the deep blue eyes? Her pulse leapt about crazily, but she made herself greet him as coolly as possible.

The party was being held at the house of one of Blair's oldest friends, Alex Hamilton, and his wife Lisa. Sian hadn't met them before, as they had been abroad.

'She's lovely, Blair,' Lisa exclaimed, as she and her husband met them at the door. 'I always had a sneaking suspicion you had a thing for redheads,' she declared once they had been divested of their coats, patting her own curls, which were only one or two shades lighter than Sian's.

Blair kissed her. 'If you hadn't been a lost cause, Lisa, my love, who knows? But then, I wouldn't have met Sian, so it's a good thing Alex had already snapped you up.'

Alex grinned. 'You never stood a chance, old son. I hope you don't mind if I kiss this extremely attractive young lady?' He didn't wait for an answer, but swept her into his arms in truly romantic, silent-screen fashion.

Laughing, Sian played up to him. Out of the corner of her eye she watched Blair for his reaction, but he merely looked amused. Her spirits sank. When Alex set her on her feet again she looked up into his charming face with its thick crop of prematurely grey hair, and caught his wink.

'You musn't mind him,' Lisa exclaimed long-sufferingly. 'He's more a shriek that a shiekh. Blair, why don't you take Valentino here and help yourselves to some drinks? I want to ask Sian where she found this divine dress.'

The men thus dismissed, Sian found herself separated from Blair and spent an amusing half-hour with Lisa before their hostess was claimed by some new arrivals. She circulated then, and was chatting with Muriel and John Adams, a couple she had met a few times, when Deanna arrived. Forgetting her escort, the blonde homed in on Blair as if answering a beacon. Sian watched as the woman drew Blair's attention and then reached up to kiss him.

Jealousy stabbed its hateful knives into her heart. However much she wanted to, she couldn't go up and kiss him the way Deanna did. What was worse, it was the sort of move she wanted to have exclusive right to. She watched rigidly as the blonde seemed to be pleading with Blair about something, and ground her teeth when he, without visible reluctance, excused himself from the group and walked away with her.

'If he's any sort of a man,' John Adams declared caustically from beside her, 'he should be finding a high place to shove her off. The fall won't hurt her, but the sudden stop at the end will either kill her or cure her. Anything less won't get through.'

Muriel studied Sian's serious face. 'It's not a case of *not* seeing the wood for the trees, but *not wanting* to,' she stated furiously.

Sian found the analogy particularly apt. 'I've been planning a spot of forest clearance myself. I hope you've no objection if I should suddenly yell "timber"!' It would afford her the greatest satisfaction.

Muriel's eyes widened. 'None at all. Blair might have other ideas,' she warned.

Right then, Sian couldn't care less what Blair's reaction would be. All her fury was turned on the blonde. Deanna had never wasted an opportunity to put the needle in, and tonight was positively the last straw. It was another of those times when her red hair ruled supreme.

The fuse ran out when the few couples still left at two in the morning were drinking coffee. Sian was chatting to Alex when she watched Blair fail to remove Deanna's hand from his arm. That was enough. Alex's only reaction to her sudden stop mid-sentence was to send out a soundless whistle. Recognising the signs from his own wife's warnings of imminent eruption, he accepted her coffee-cup with a silent laugh and watched her walk away.

Approaching the objects of her anger, Sian gave no thought to what anyone would think. Coming to a halt, she picked up Deanna's hand and dropped it away as if it was something nasty the cat had dragged in.

'*Will* you stop pawing at him?' she snapped, aware that all conversation had rather dramatically stopped.

For an instant Deanna looked taken aback, then she laughed. 'Blair doesn't mind.'

'Maybe he doesn't,' Sian returned, throwing Blair a withering look. 'But I do. It's nauseating watching you throw yourself about as if you were some sex-starved adolescent!' It was over the top, but in her temper she didn't care.

Somewhere in the room, someone gasped at that.

'What did you say?' Deanna gasped, looking as if she couldn't believe her ears. 'How dare you?'

Sian's hands went to her hips. 'I dare, because Blair happens to be my fiancé, not yours. And if you keep this up, you'll find I dare more than that. For hours I've put up with you, but enough's enough. The joke's wearing awfully thin.'

Deanna had high flags of colour in her cheeks. 'A joke, is it? I'll give you a joke.' She turned to Blair, clutching his arm. 'Tell her, darling, tell her it's really me you want.'

Blair had been watching Sian with an odd light in his eyes and a smile hovering on his lips, but now he turned to Deanna and removed her hands gently. 'But I can't, because it wouldn't be true.' To give him his due, he said it kindly enough.

All Deanna's confidence evaporated at that. 'No! That's not true. You only asked her to marry you because you were angry with me!'

'Blair didn't do the proposing, Deanna, I did,' Sian told her flatly, her temper-bubble pricked, and beginning to feel very sick at her own behaviour.

'And I accepted,' Blair added gently, placing an arm across Deanna's shoulders, but the woman flung it off.

'You bastard!' she choked, and her hand connected with Blair's cheek with a sound like a pistol-shot. 'I'll make you sorry for this, both of you.' With angry strides she dashed from the room, followed by a grimacing Alex, whose voice could be heard trying to placate just before the front door slammed, rocking the building.

Angry at herself now too, Sian turned on Blair who was nursing his cheek. 'I hope you're satisfied!' she drawled, icily furious, totally uncaring of their audience still avidly listening.

Blair wasn't bothered by them, either. 'Are we going to have another scene now?' he asked in amused curiosity.

Sian's temper went through the roof again, but she was also only a centimetre away from tears of remorse. 'I hate you. I detest you. You're the most loathsome person I know!' she hissed, her hands clenched into angry fists.

Blair had the utter gall to start grinning. 'Darling, our friends are getting anxious. They don't know you as I do. They think you mean it.'

'Well, I do! I'm not backing down,' she declared.

His hands fastened on her shoulders, his grin broadening. 'If you won't back down, you'll have to back out, because we're leaving,' he said facetiously, propelling her backwards to the door, followed by relieved laughter from the others.

In the hall he let her go and turned to Alex and Lisa, who had followed them out.

'Well!' Lisa gasped. 'We'll be dining out on that scene for a long time.'

By this time Sian was beginning to feel quite dreadful about the whole scene. 'Oh, God, I'm so sorry about that,' she groaned.

'Nonsense! I could sit through it all again,' Alex comforted her. 'It's probably unkind, but Dee had that coming. She left here like a bat out of hell, nearly took my hand off in the process.'

'Alex is right,' Lisa added. 'Although you're as much at fault for leading Dee on, Blair. You know she's blind where you're concerned. I'll give her a ring in the morning, just to make sure she's all right.'

'I stand rebuked,' Blair said, helping a much subdued Sian into her coat. 'Both you and Sian can't be wrong. Goodnight, Lisa, my love. I'll be seeing you, Alex.'

Sian found herself having to say her farewells as he bustled her down the steps. In the car, Blair started to laugh. Sian stared at him in icy silence. When he sobered, he took one look at her set face and put the car in motion.

'I didn't know you had such a temper. Are you going to tell me why you were so angry?' he asked quietly after a while.

Sian rubbed her fingers wearily over her forehead. 'I don't know. It seemed like a good idea at the time.'

There was a small silence while Blair negotiated a double-parked car.

'You have no need to be jealous of Dee,' he told her shockingly.

'I wasn't!' she gasped out defensively, realising just what her outburst must have revealed.

Blair sighed, but kept his eyes on the road. 'Sian, we have to talk—*I* have to talk. When we get you home, I'm coming in.'

She had no idea what he could be going to say, unless it was to break off the engagement at last. She cursed her unruly tongue and sat beside him in an agony of suspense as they travelled the last few miles.

Once inside her flat, she stood by nervously as Blair paced to the window and stood staring out. She slipped off her coat, laying it over a chair, then, crossing her arms protectively over her stomach, she watched him.

Blair's shoulders rose and fell as he took a deep sigh. 'Did you ever wonder why I hated you so much?' he asked flatly.

Sian frowned. 'I thought it was because of Neal. He was your friend and I hurt him.'

'That was part of it, but not all. I hated you because I wanted you for myself.' He turned to face her then, blue eyes fixing compellingly on her face.

Sian's brain reeled. 'What?'

'Neal sent me a photograph of you,' he went on doggedly. 'I wanted you then and hated myself for it. You were Neal's, and off limits to me. I valued his friendship and nothing would make me betray it. Then I came home from the States and found out what you had done to him. That's when I started to hate you— because even then I still wanted you. I've never stopped. It was easy to subdue while I was still bound on revenge, but then you confessed the truth to me. That changed everything. I had no reason to hate you any more, and no reason to expect you to want to deepen our relationship. I was determined to give you your freedom.'

Sian could scarcely take it all in. 'Was?' she croaked.

Blair moved away from the window then and came towards her. 'Tonight, for the first time, I realised that perhaps you didn't want me to let you go. Am I right?'

In an instinctive move for self-preservation, she opened her mouth to say no, then stopped. Blair had been honest, and she owed him that too. Besides, she was so close to getting what she really wanted, it was ridiculous to let pride stand in her way. Wanting might not be loving, but it was a start. Even the longest journeys started with one small step.

'Yes,' she conceded, her voice a wobbly whisper.

His face had been austere, but now, as he reached out to take her gently by the shoulders, a slow smile chased away the harsh lines. 'Then I'll keep you,' he said softly.

He drew her into his arms and she went easily, her breath leaving her in a shaky sigh. Her arms slid about him and they stood like that for a moment or two, drinking in the unexpected closeness. Beneath her ear she could hear Blair's heart thudding out a rapid tattoo, an echo of her own.

The soft kisses that rained down on her hair had her tipping her head up like a flower towards the sun. Warm lips brushed over forehead and eyes in a gentle caress that matched the soothing stroke of his hand on her back. Each touch was a subtle restitution for the past, and her heart sang. She was shrouded in a blissful serenity, but not for long. Gradually his caresses evoked new and delicious sensations that chased their way across her skin and sent arrows of flame down through her body to kindle flash fires there.

A sighing moan left her parted lips as she tipped her head back to allow him freer access to her throat. Strong arms gathered her close to his lean, firm body, and she discovered for herself just how much he wanted her.

Blair lifted his head to gaze down into her upturned face. Blue eyes sent her a scorching message. 'I want to love you,' he declared roughly. It was a question too, offering her the right to say no. Only there was no thought of refusal in Sian's mind.

'Yes,' she assented huskily.

That was all the encouragement Blair needed. He sought her mouth in a series of teasing kisses that drove her wild. Lips and teeth eased her lips apart then took possession, and hungrily she responded. The room—everything—faded in the face of the shivering delight he evoked with breathtaking mastery. She could only respond, and she did so with all the generosity of an un-tried spirit.

The settee was beside them and they sank on to it. Drugged by a passion that took her strength away and returned it twofold, she moaned when Blair sat up away from her. The flame in his eyes transfixed her. She had never seen such naked desire on a man's face before, but it didn't scare her. She thrilled at the knowledge that she could arouse so strong-willed a man, and her stomach twisted on a hot, sweet ache.

Shrugging out of his coat, Blair tugged at his tie and discarded it. Seconds later his shirt followed. He reached for her then, binding her to him in a deep searing kiss. It was as if a dam had burst, and there was no power on earth that could stop the force of their need.

Beneath her fingers Blair's skin was scorching. Ten-tatively at first, and then with increasing confidence, she explored him. Fingertips felt out every tensed muscle, every indentation of his spine, glorying in a freedom so long denied. She tasted his sigh as she found the pleasure-points, delighting as he shuddered beneath her tactile exploration. As his kiss probed deeper into the honeyed cavern she opened to him, her fingers splayed across his back, flexing, pressing harder in an effort to possess yet more of him.

Blair's weight pushed her down into the cushions, strong hands seeking the fastenings of her dress, dealing with them expertly, until with a groan of satisfaction he could peel the bodice away from her and close one hand about her breast and bring it up to meet his descending mouth. In a paroxysm of pleasure, Sian arched closer to that tortuous delight. To the tongue that circled and stroked, the teeth that nipped and the lips that suckled until she groaned and gasped, fingers locking in his hair to hold him closer. When he transferred his attention to the twin globe with its jutting peak, she thought she would die.

He was worshipping her body, and she wanted to do the same to him. Her mouth sought his shoulder, the only part of him she could reach, lips parting to press moist kisses feverishly across his flesh. She tasted him— the clean scent of cologne and the salty tang of sweat as their skin began to glow with a moist heat.

But Blair didn't stop at her breasts. As his hands tugged her dress down over her hips, taking all she wore beneath with it, his lips blazed a trail down her ivory velvet skin. The reverence of that exploration took her breath away and left no space for embarrassment. His lips felt the knocking of her heart as they undulated over her ribs, started fluttering nerves in the gentle slope of her belly. Calmed the frantic arch of her hips as they roved the subtle V of her thighs, and brought a gasp to her lips as they discovered the sensitive skin behind her knees.

Sian hadn't dreamt, couldn't have known, that she could feel this way. When Blair stood up to lift her into his arms, she was a mass of tingling, receptive nerves. There was a hectic flush on Blair's cheeks as he gazed down at her, then she slid her arms about his neck, burying her lips against the thudding pulse at his throat.

In her bedroom, beside her bed, Blair let her glide downwards until her toes touched the ground, kissing her with long, drugging kisses that built a need his strong hands and arms stoked with endless caresses. Sian clung on as the world began to revolve around her. His arms were straining her closer even as hers were striving to do, their two hearts beating out one pagan melody.

With a groan, Blair tore his mouth from hers, easing her away and down on to the cool sheets that had no power to ease the heat from her limbs. She felt fluid, her eyes glittering as she unashamedly watched him remove the last of his clothes.

'You're beautiful.' Husky with passion, she breathed the words.

Tall and strong, his body glistened in the pale light of the moon through the windows. Oh, she loved him so— wanted him so desperately. And he wanted her. There was no hiding it, and she was proud of it. Proud that she could bring him to this. Proud that he was so male. Proud that he was hers.

Sian held her hand out to him and he came down to her, pressing her into the softness with his weight.

'I'm not beautiful, you are,' he muttered thickly, his eyes staring hotly into hers. 'Exquisite. Perfect. Made for me.'

Glistening limbs entangled and held as they strained ever closer, stoking a fire that made them both moan and tremble, sigh and beg. Inexperienced though she was, by instinct Sian knew how to please him. With her lips and hands she gave measure for measure, and every caress she received from him built up the tension within her until she was writhing in abandon, begging without words for the final act that would make them one.

When he eased over her, parting her thighs with his, she was ready for him. His hands framed her hips, lifting her to join him, his body coming into hers with a strong thrust, only to freeze as the brief moment of pain made her tense and cry out. Blair groaned, raising himself on arms that quivered, to look down into her face with disbelief. But the moment had passed, the memory of it fading as she gloried in the feel of him within her.

'Sian?'

He sounded shocked, uncertain, and her heart swelled. All the certainty of her womanhood was in her touch as she pulled him down to her, her hands gliding to his hips to hold him closer as she began to move beneath him.

'Don't stop,' she breathed against his lips.

Blair couldn't fight her and his own need, and, burying his face in her neck, he started to move again. Slowly at first, as if afraid she might cry out, but when she only welcomed his ever-deepening thrusts, the tempo quickened. The spiral of tension was growing now as she matched his rhythm, climbing and climbing until the summit was reached, and she did cry out, hearing her own name echoing in her ears as Blair joined her in that white-hot explosion of pleasure.

Sian abandoned herself to his arms as she took that first glide down through galaxies of delight. Blair was a pleasurable weight upon her, but there came a moment when he sighed and moved away. She sighed too, as a delicious wave of languor took her ever closer towards sleep. Curling into his side, she rested her chin on his arm.

'Blair,' she murmured softly.

His arm closed about her. 'Don't talk,' he whispered, his voice sounding gravelly, as if it was out of practice. 'Sleep now, we'll talk tomorrow.'

Content with that, she smiled sleepily and was asleep almost at once.

Blair didn't close his eyes. He slanted his head down so that he could see her. Frowning heavily, his hand came up to play with one damp red curl. He allowed his head to fall back on the pillow, but still he didn't sleep; instead he stared unseeingly up into the darkness.

# CHAPTER EIGHT

SIAN came awake with the pain of bright sunlight in her eyes, and groaned. She groaned again when twisting away from that light had her muscles protesting. Memory returned and she gave a catlike smile and stretched languorously. Making love with Blair had been the ultimate experience. She was confident she had pleased him too. He had been all hers, and her love had deepened. She wondered idly if he realised she loved him. He knew now that he had been her first lover, and she knew he was astute enough to put two and two together and come up with the right answer. She found she was too happy to care that her secret was out.

She reached for him then, and to her alarm found only cold, empty sheet. She sat up in a hurry, flicking tumbled red locks back out of her eyes, careless of the duvet slipping down to her waist. Her eyes flew to the clock, discovering it was still early yet. She couldn't see a trace of his clothes, nor was there any sound from the bathroom.

Fear clutched icily at her stomach. He had gone. She sat there stunned, trying to work out what had happened. Trying not to panic. When the bedroom door slowly opened and a towel-draped Blair backed into the room, she was shocked. Then, as he turned, holding a tray on which sat two steaming cups of coffee, her head swam and she quickly dropped her head to hold off the dizziness.

The bed dipped as he sat down beside her. 'Hey, what is it?' He must have set the tray down, because he took her shoulders in both hands.

Sian had to swallow to find her voice. 'I thought you'd gone,' she explained gruffly.

She found herself pulled up against his strong, hair-roughened chest, and slipped her hands around him, holding on tight.

'Without a word? After last night?' he queried, running an exploratory hand down her spine.

Sian shivered, a mixture of delight and remembered anxiety. 'You wouldn't have had a qualm before,' she said, looking up at him, and was surprised to find him looking discomfited.

'But things aren't the same, are they?' he insisted. His blue eyes seemed to be trying to probe into her very soul, as if in search of an answer to an unspecified question.

She smiled to reassure his doubts. 'I hope not.'

Blair heaved a deep sigh and moved to rest back against the headboard, drawing Sian across his lap and into the shelter of his arms. 'Are you happy?' he questioned softly.

'Yes.' She sighed contentedly.

His eyes roved her with a lazy warmth and lit on a faint bruise on her breast. He touched it gently. 'Did I hurt you last night?' he asked broodingly.

Sian ran a hand over his bristly chin and smiled. 'You might look like a pirate this morning, but you didn't behave like one last night.'

'Why didn't you tell me you were a virgin?'

'You didn't ask me,' she said simply.

Blair's jaw tightened. 'Yet you knew I believed you'd had other lovers,' he persisted.

'Would you have believed me if I'd told you you were wrong?'

'Probably not,' he admitted ruefully. 'Why no lovers, Sian? You're a desirable woman.'

She lowered her lashes. 'Sleeping around never appealed to me. Besides...' She broke off wistfully.

'Besides, what?' he urged.

She swallowed. 'I was too scared of hurting anyone else like I hurt Neal. Scared of the responsibility in a close relationship.'

Blair frowned. 'What happened to change your mind last night?'

Sian gave that a lot of thought before answering. 'I think I realised that all men aren't as vulnerable as Neal. I believe I loved him then, but he was weak.'

'But you don't love him now?'

She looked at him sadly. 'There will always be a place for him in my heart, but it doesn't come close to the way I feel...' She broke off with a soft gasp, realising just what she was saying.

There was an odd light in Blair's eyes as he said, 'The way you feel about me?'

Sian stared at him and knew there was simply no going back. The Rubicon had been left far behind. 'Blair, I...' His finger on her lips halted the words.

He shook his head. 'You don't have to say anything,' he declared swiftly. As if he didn't *want* her to say it.

She pulled his hand away gently, her sapphire eyes steadfast. 'You know I love you, don't you?' she stated frankly.

He had gone quite still. 'Sian, I...' It was her turn to stop his lips.

'I don't expect anything of you, Blair, especially not the words if you don't mean them. This is enough for me.' It wasn't true, of course, but she wanted his honesty, not his lies. His desire was honest.

She had never seen him look so uncomfortable, and a little anger surfaced. 'I don't want pity, Blair.'

He stared down at her as if he had found he was holding a totally different woman, and shook his head a little as if to clear it. 'What do you want then, Sian?' he asked with unaccustomed tenderness.

She knew the answer to that. 'I want to make love with you,' she said simply.

Blair reacted to that with a swiftness that took her breath away. Rolling over, he captured her beneath him. 'Now that,' he said with a smile, 'is something I'll be

only too happy to oblige you with.' So saying, he brought
his lips down masterfully on hers.

They made love with none of the urgency of the night
before, but with a burning, languorous passion that took
them higher than before. Later they showered, then Sian
left Blair to use her razor again while she prepared
breakfast. By tacit agreement, nothing more had been
said of her admission that she loved him. She wasn't
sorry she had told him, although it wasn't the sort of
information she would ever have dared tell the old Blair.

She had told him too, that what they had now would
be enough, and she would make it so. She had waited
all her life for a love like this, and she wasn't about to
give it up before she had to. Besides, if the age of miracles
wasn't past, he could come to love her—but she wasn't
going to hang her hopes on that.

They were late for work but no one noticed. Once again
the atmosphere in the office changed. All the business
was dealt with in the usual way, but now, whenever she
found his eyes on her, they contained neither anger nor
indifference. They could joke now and exchange intimate, knowing glances that, for Sian, made the
workload easier to handle.

That evening they ate at Blair's apartment. Sian was
glad. She didn't want to share him with a whole restaurant full of people where he could be recognised and
they would have to be polite when what they really
wanted was to be alone.

After they had eaten, Sian curled up beside him on
the couch. Sighing contentedly, she surveyed the cold
beauty of the décor.

'You know, all this room really needs is a coat of warm
paint, even some paper on one wall,' she decided aloud.

'That's all, is it?' Blair enquired in amusement.

Her expression became thoughtful as she warmed to
her theme. 'Well, no, not all. The furniture is OK, so is
the carpet, but those windows need full draw curtains,

not blinds. Then if you had a sofa-table behind us with a lamp, that would make this part of the room cosy, especially in winter. And you need plants and more cushions,' she enthused.

Blair had followed her pointing finger as she spoke. Now he looked down at her animated face. 'All right, I'll make a deal with you. You move in here and I'll let you redecorate,' he proposed immediately.

She swivelled to look at him. 'You're not serious?'

Blue eyes twinkled. 'Of course I am. I told you ages ago that my mother thought it looked cold. I've always agreed. I simply never had enough interest to do anything about it.'

'I didn't mean that and you know it,' she charged in exasperation. 'Blair, be serious for a minute. You can't really want me to move in.'

'I would hardly have suggested it if I didn't mean it,' he replied simply.

She wanted to, but still she hesitated. 'It's a big step,' she said slowly.

Blair cupped her face. 'I know. How can I persuade you?' He didn't take his eyes off her as he started to speak carefully. 'What we have going between us isn't something I believe will die out in a matter of days. I don't want to spend just the odd night with you here or at your flat. We need time together. We need to make this a relationship, and not some hole and corner affair. I know that's not what you want.'

Of course it wasn't. She was simply suffering from a belated attack of nerves. She really wanted to be with him, to share his life for as long as she could.

'All right,' she agreed breathlessly, and her heart skipped a beat as he smiled.

'Good.' Suddenly he laughed low in his throat, and she looked at him in puzzlement. He enlightened her. 'This isn't the only room, you know. I need your opinion on the others. Why don't we start in the master bedroom?'

That slow fire started to burn at the look in his eyes. 'What a good idea,' she agreed, and allowed him to pull her to her feet.

It wasn't surprising that the bedroom was the only room they got around to that night.

Sian moved in over the next few days. She was keeping her own flat on, because common sense said she might need it one day. Once her personal possessions had been dotted about the apartment, she felt as if she had never lived anywhere else.

The days that followed were the happiest of Sian's life. Sharing with Blair was exciting. Even cooking a meal was an adventure. She felt as if she fell more deeply in love by the hour. They laughed, argued and made love in an atmosphere she had never experienced before. Life at home had never had this warmth. She knew she could be asking to be hurt worse than she ever had before, but it was a risk she was prepared to take.

They did the decorating together. Sian's experience was limited and Blair's virtually non-existent, but he caught her enthusiasm and set to with a will. It was slow going, especially when it was interrupted for kisses that often got out of hand, but worth it. They would fall into bed pleasantly exhausted, but never too tired not to make slow and wonderful love to each other.

Life couldn't have been more perfect. Blair seemed really happy, and unrecognisable from the man she had met in the lift not so very long ago. She never asked him how he felt about her. She knew he cared and that made her content.

Then one morning at breakfast he seemed rather preoccupied. Sian watched him carefully but said nothing, knowing he would tell her about it in his own good time if he wanted to.

She reached out to collect his empty cup and went to refill it from the pot on the counter. She had thought he was still miles away when she brought the now full cup back, and gasped as Blair relieved her of it and pulled her down on to his lap. He buried his lips against the perfumed warmth of her neck with a soft groan, and she shivered. She could feel his reluctance as he eased himself away.

'There's a strong possibility I might have to fly to the States this evening,' he told her.

'Oh, no!' she wailed. 'Why didn't you tell me before?'

'Because it still might not happen. It all depends on my meeting today.'

Sian knew the one he meant, and knew she should have realised the possibility herself. She tried hard to hide her sudden dejection. 'Oh, well, it can't be helped. If you do go, will it be for long?'

Blair sighed. 'I really couldn't say.' He gave her a long, hard, frowning look. 'I'm not looking forward to going, that's for certain. I'd rather be here with you.'

Warm fingers curled about her heart. 'I'll miss you,' she whispered huskily.

Their eyes met and held.

'I'm amazed there was ever a time when I didn't love you,' he declared gruffly.

The world tilted alarmingly. 'Blair...' Her voice was almost non-existent.

His brows rose. 'Hmm?'

She clutched at his shoulders. 'Oh, God, don't tease me! Did you mean it?'

His face was very serious suddenly. 'I think so.'

Sian wound her arms around his neck. 'Oh, hold me. I think I'm dying!'

His head lowered and his lips plundered her neck. 'No one dies of love, darling, only loving, and then only a little death,' he declared huskily, and trailed butterfly kisses up until he could reach her lips, and his kiss then was everything she could ever have hoped for.

With a low groan, Blair eased away. 'Come back to bed with me,' he demanded thickly.

She wanted to, really wanted to, but...'We'll be late again,' she sighed as his lips began to plunder down to the scented valley of her breasts.

'Shower with me, then,' he urged roughly, loosening the tie belt of her robe and easing his hands inside to discover the warm curves of her body.

Sian trembled and her legs suddenly seemed unable to bear her weight. 'Yes,' she sighed weakly, reaching for him with eager hands.

'Afterwards,' Blair moaned, and, sweeping her up into his arms, carried her back to the bedroom.

Blair flew to the States that evening. Sian didn't go to the airport to see him off because he had asked her not to. She argued, but eventually gave in. The minute he walked out of the door she began missing him. The apartment seemed so empty and lifeless. She knew it wouldn't change until he came back. It wasn't fair that he had had to go away so soon after telling her he loved her, but at least she had that memory to keep her warm at night.

It was the longest week on record, feeling like a year by the time it was over. When she finally heard his key in the door on Friday night, she fairly flew into the hallway, then stopped and took one deep, thankful breath. Blair straightened from setting down his case and saw her standing there.

For countless seconds he simply stood there staring at her, the oddest expression on his face, then he smiled and opened his arms, and she flew into them. There was an intensity in his kiss, almost desperation as he strained her closer. She more than matched him, and when finally they drew apart, both were breathing unsteadily.

'I missed you,' he declared, almost wonderingly.

She gave a throaty laugh. 'There's no need to sound so surprised. I missed you too, you know.'

His eyes searched hers. 'Did you?' he murmured huskily.

She closed her eyes and pressed her cheek against him. 'Oh, yes. Never doubt it. I love you.' She expected to hear him tell her he loved her, too. When he didn't, she pulled back in surprise, frowning at him. 'Blair?' He looked quite grim for a moment, and her nerves leapt in alarm.

He came to with a start, and only then smiled at her. 'I'm sorry, sweetheart—of course I love you. I'm just not used to saying it yet. Forgive me?'

Her smile was wobbly with relief. 'Of course I do. Have you had dinner? I could make you something if you want it,' she offered as he placed an arm over her shoulder and they walked into the lounge.

Blair tugged at his tie. 'I ate on the plane, but I could do with some coffee. Need any help?'

She pushed him down on to the couch. 'Hardly. You put your feet up. I won't be a minute.'

In the kitchen she pondered his strange behaviour, then dismissed it with a shrug. Jet-lag, probably. It did funny things to people. She made the coffee and carried it through, sitting beside him on the couch while they drank it.

'How was it over there? Did you get everything sorted out?' she asked after the silence had dragged on long enough to become uncomfortable.

Blair frowned. 'What? Oh, yes. Yes, it was fine. We now have a contract worth hundreds of thousands of dollars.'

Sian smiled. 'Good. At least that means it was worth being without you for a week.'

'Hmm?' he asked absently.

She gave him a sympathetic look. 'Poor Blair, you really are tired, aren't you?'

He set his cup down with a heavy sigh. 'Actually, you're right. So, if you have no objections, I plan to take a shower and crash out for the next eight hours.' He rose as he said it, giving her a brief glance before leaving the room.

Sian stared after him, lips parted in soundless astonishment. He had been so abrupt, it was almost as if... Dear God, he wasn't regretting asking her to move in already? Anguish twisted at her heart. She got a grip on herself before panic set in. She was just being fanciful, that was all. He was tired, anyone would be after that long haul.

Yet when she went into the bedroom later to get ready for bed, his back was resolutely turned from her side of the bed. She knew instinctively he was only pretending to be asleep. Something was wrong, very wrong. She showered in a state of deepening agitation, and returned to the bedroom.

Discarding her robe over a chair, she slipped into the bed beside him. She could feel the invisible wall between them and knew she must knock it down and discover the truth. Sliding closer, she put her arm around him. His flinch drove a dagger into her heart, and she rolled away again, biting her lip as sudden tears stung her eyes.

'Blair, tell me what's wrong. What have I done?' she challenged into the darkness.

Blair gave a restless sigh and turned on to his back. 'You haven't done anything,' he said heavily.

'But? There's a but in there somewhere. I can hear it, sense it. But what, Blair?' she demanded unevenly.

He rolled over on to his side to look down at her. 'But nothing, Sian. I'm just tired. I packed a lot of work into a short number of hours. Added to which...' He hesitated a moment before adding, 'I missed you more than I thought it possible.'

Pained eyes stared at him. 'And you don't like it, do you? You're having second thoughts.'

'I've had second, third and fourth thoughts. I'm only human. The result is that I'm here and you're here—right where I want you to be.'

Sian closed her eyes and swallowed painfully. 'Blair, I don't want to lose you. You scared me. You were so...so...'

'Shh!' He placed a finger over her lips. 'I know. I'm sorry.' He punctuated the apology with kisses that gradually deepened, until with a groan he pulled her into his arms.

All her doubts were swept away on the tide of his love-making. Yet a long time after she had at last fallen asleep, Blair lay wakeful beside her.

The ringing of the telephone woke her next morning. Blinking owlishly, she clung on to Blair as he moved to lift the receiver.

'Hello?' His voice still sounded thick with sleep. 'Yes...yes...that's right...Who did you say this is?' His voice was much brisker all of a sudden, as his attention was caught. 'All right, I understand. Go ahead.' There was a long pause then, as the caller explained the reason for the call. 'Yes, I understand. You did your best. We'll be there as soon as we can. Goodbye.' Blair put the receiver back on the cradle and looked down at her raised face. He wasn't smiling, and her heart dropped like a stone.

'What is it?' she gasped, sitting up.

He sat up, too. 'Bad news, I'm afraid.'

She gave him an agonised look. 'Oh, Blair, not your parents!'

'Not mine, no,' he said slowly. 'I'm afraid it's your father. There's just no easy way for me to say this. He had a stroke. He died four days ago.'

It was a tremendous shock. She could never have imagined how much. All these years she had hated him, yet still deep within her was the little girl who had wanted to be loved and couldn't understand why she wasn't. Now it was too late.

As the first hoarse sob left her, Blair drew her into his arms, cradling her there. The tears came from no-where. She didn't even know if she was crying for her father or herself. It got all mixed up. Through it all,

Blair held her. It took a long time before she was calm again and could think.

'Who was that on the phone?' she asked wearily.

'The housekeeper. She's been trying to contact you for days, apparently, and only belatedly thought of trying to contact me. The funeral's today, Sian. I said we'd try and make it.'

She raked her hair back with her fingers in a weary gesture. 'Yes. Yes, I suppose we should,' she agreed dully. She slid off the bed to her feet.

He watched her carefully for a moment before getting up, too. 'You'd better pack a case. We'll have to stay the night.'

'All right.' She nodded and disappeared into the bathroom.

The shower did her a world of good. The unexpected storm of grief had passed, leaving her cleansed. She knew she would cry no more tears for the man who had given her scant affection during his lifetime. She would go to his funeral and say her last farewell, and then it would be over. Her future lay with Blair, and their love for each other.

It was a solemn journey, neither speaking very much. Sian was content simply to listen to a tape. She was glad Blair was with her. She could feel his sympathy and support, and it was a benison. Before, she had suffered everything alone, but she wasn't going to be alone ever again.

The service was almost over when they arrived at the church. There was a large group of mourners about the grave, for Sir Rhodri had been an important man in the area. Aware of being the cynosure of all eyes, Sian took her place beside Mrs Huntly. The old housekeeper was visibly upset. Sian slipped her arm through the other woman's. The housekeeper had never approved of Sir Rhodri's treatment of his daughter, and had done her best to alleviate it. When Sian had been driven to leave, she had stayed on at the house out of family loyalty. Whatever the past, she still grieved.

It was soon over, and slowly the mourners began to drift away. Sian was compelled to thank everyone for coming because it was expected, though she was conscious that many here would be cynical about her late arrival, and deeming her presence had only been induced out of avarice.

Mrs Huntly went back to the house with Sian and Blair. The two women sat in the back of the car, talking in hushed voices, renewing an affection that bridged years of silence.

It was odd for Sian to return to the house she had grown up in after all these years. The coldness was still there in the high-ceilinged rooms with their wainscoting and leaded windows. That vital spark of human warmth that turned four walls into a home had always been missing. She felt like a stranger, an interloper, but then her personality had scarcely been allowed to imprint itself here.

For the next hour she was kept occupied in talking to all the people who had come to pay their last respects. Through it all, she was conscious of Blair not very far away, giving her his moral support. Finally, everyone left except those few who had been summoned to the reading of the will.

It wasn't a long document. The bulk of the property had been left to her, with sizeable bequests to the staff and various charities. That she was now a wealthy woman meant nothing to Sian. Money had been her father's god, not hers. As for his business, she intended to ask Blair's advice about that as soon as possible.

When the front door was closed for the last time, Sian breathed a sigh of relief. She went over to where Blair stood and slipped her arm around his waist, getting comfort from resting her head on his chest.

'You were marvellous,' she said softly. 'Thank you for being here.'

'Where else would I be?' he queried gruffly.

She smiled and tipped her head up to him. 'Would you mind very much if I left you just for a little? I want to talk to Mrs H.'

Blair dropped a soft kiss on her lips. 'Go ahead. I'll be OK.'

Sian found the older woman in her sitting-room at the back of the house. With a fond smile, she hugged the ample frame that had been a comfort to her years ago.

'How are you, Mrs H?' Their conversation earlier had dwelt mainly on her father's stroke and the house-keeper's attempts to get hold of Sian.

The woman patted her hand. 'I'm fine, Miss Sian. Save for me rheumatics. You're looking bonny. I was right happy to hear about your young man. He looks good for you, that one,' she pronounced judicially.

'I hope so.' Sian grinned. 'What will you do now, Mrs H? Now that Father's gone?' she asked in concern.

'Oh, don't you go worrying yourself over me, lass. It's already arranged. I'm going to stay with my sister in Ventnor. She runs a guest house, so I can be a hand to her now we're both getting on a bit. It's you I was worried about, but now I've seen him, it's put my mind at rest.'

'I'm glad you like him. Father did, too.' She frowned over that.

Mrs Huntly gave her a speaking look. 'We buried the past today, lass. You cut along to your future. That's my advice. That's where you want to be now, not talking to an old 'un like me. By the by, I made up the bed in your old room. If you want to make up another for your young man, that's up to you. Personally, I reckon you'll be right cosy in there together,' she finished with a twinkle in her eye.

Sian blushed and laughed. 'You're a terror. What will we do with you?'

'Send me an invitation to the wedding.'

Sian kissed her cheek. 'That's a promise. Bless you, Mrs H. Without you...'

'Oh, tush!' the housekeeper snapped, brushing at her eyes. 'Just you be off now and leave me to get the dinner on.'

Sian obeyed, wiping her own eyes.

The three of them ate their dinner in the kitchen. The dining-room was far too formal. Besides, somehow the general atmosphere of the house didn't percolate back here, and they could laugh without feeling guilty.

'When are you going to go through your father's things?' the housekeeper asked after the dishes had been cleared away.

Sian looked at her in dismay. 'I thought you had done it.' She didn't welcome the idea at all.

'I've been through his clothes, lass, but all his personal things were in the study. I didn't think it right to touch those.'

Sian bit her lip. 'Well, I suppose it's got to be done,' she decided slowly.

'We'll do it now,' Blair offered, capturing her hand. 'I'll help.'

'Would you?' She smiled her relief.

'Come on.' Blair stood up and pulled her to her feet. 'It's better to get it over with.'

'I'll bring you some coffee,' the housekeeper called after their departing figures.

Sian had rarely ventured into the room at the back of the house. When she had, it had usually meant a lecture on her behaviour. It was a large room, well lit, with books lining the walls and comfortable furniture. A fire had been set in the grate, and Blair put a match to it. All the same, Sian shivered.

'Where do we start?'

Blair took a swift look round. 'The desk, I suppose.'

They set to at once. There were papers everywhere, and they all had to be looked at. It looked as if it would

take days to make head or tail of it all. They were glad
of the coffee when Mrs Huntly brought it in.

'Did he have a safe?' Blair asked a little later.

Sian looked up. 'Yes, behind the Turner. The com-
bination was his birthday, unless he changed it.' She gave
him the figures and they proved to be still correct, for
within minutes the door swung back. She returned to
the papers she held while Blair delved inside.

'Hmm. There are some boxes of jewellery. Your
mother's, presumably. Some bonds and certificates.
What's this? Some old newspaper cuttings. Good God!
They're forty years old! There are some folders, too. Let
me see. This one seems to be about...' He stopped
speaking with a suddenness that echoed.

Sian had only been listening to him with half an ear.
It took her a second or two to realise he had stopped
talking, and then she did look up. Blair was frozen to
the spot, head bent over something he held in his hand.

'Blair?' When she received no reply, she stood up
quickly. 'What is it?' she demanded sharply.

He looked round then, and his face was ashen. Her
heart twisted in anxiety. He looked as if he were dreadfully ill.

'Dear God! I thought you were lying!' The words
seemed to be dragged out of him.

She picked up his agony and started to tremble herself.
Her legs felt boneless as she came round the desk to
him. 'What do you mean?' She took the folder from his
nerveless fingers and he turned away, raking his hands
down his face.

A sick dread started to churn in her stomach as she
looked down at the folder. It only needed one look to
tell her it was the same folder the lawyer had shown her
five years ago. The one she had told Blair about that
night at his parents' house. The one in the story he had
said he believed—but now he was telling her he had really
believed she was lying.

The truth was a sledge-hammer in her chest. It had all been one horribly monstrous lie! He hadn't changed at all. He had simply found another way to make her admit she loved him, and so pay the dreadful price of his revenge!

'No!' It was the cry of a wounded animal as its heart was torn asunder. 'Oh, God! *Oh, God!*' The pain was unbearable.

Blair turned as she stumbled away, trying to get out of the room. He moved much too fast for her, catching her and holding on tight. His face was awful.

'How could I know?' he demanded hoarsely. 'How could anyone believe that a man would do such a thing, let alone a father to his own daughter?'

She was shaking so much, she could hardly speak. 'Because I told you what he was like! I told you, damn you!' she cried in a voice of utter despair.

'What's going on here?' It was Mrs Huntly, her face creased in concern.

Neither of them had heard her arrive, but her voice broke Blair's hold on her, and Sian used it to thrust him away and run from the room. She didn't stop running until she had reached her room and locked the door behind her. Tears were streaming down her face, sobs racking her frame. Pain cut through her, tearing her to shreds. The sense of betrayal was devastating. Blair didn't love her. He never had. It was all designed to punish her for Neal's death.

The enormity of the treachery drove through her on a wave of sickness, and her stomach heaved. She barely made it to the bathroom in time. She retched until long after there was anything left to bring up. Weak tears fell down her cheeks when at last she stopped, and she sank back against the tiled wall, sobbing wildly. Lacerated emotions drove her to curl her arms about her waist, as if that could numb the pain. Nothing could do that.

'Oh, God! How I hate him!'

She felt stripped of all pride. More vulnerable now than she had ever been in her life before. Not even her guilt and grief for Neal had produced this desolation of the spirit. No one had been able to destroy her as Blair had done.

Feeling so icy cold she couldn't keep a limb still, Sian finally dragged herself to her feet. She stumbled to the bed and lay down on it, drawing the covers up tight.

Painful memories racked their way through her mind. How could she have been so wrong? She would have bet all she owned and more that he had been telling the truth. Yet by his own admission he had lied. How she loathed and despised him for what he had done! He didn't deserve that she should love him!

Which had the tears falling again, because the tragedy of it was, she did love him, and probably would till the day she died.

# CHAPTER NINE

SIAN must have fallen asleep, because the sound of someone tapping on the door woke her.

'Who is it?' Her voice sounded dry, unused.

'Blair. Let me in, Sian. I have to talk to you.'

She closed her eyes on a fresh wave of pain. 'Go away! I don't ever want to see you again!'

'I'm quite prepared to break the damn door down if you don't let me in,' he threatened.

She believed him. With lips drawn tight, she flung back the covers and went to unlock the door. She moved away immediately, folding her arms protectively across her chest, hands rubbing up and down her arms.

Blair walked slowly into the room, eyeing her white face and reddened eyes grimly. In her turn, she studied him. He still had no colour and his face looked gaunt. A flicker of compassion smote her, but she quelled it ruthlessly.

'Well? Say what you have to say and get out,' she ordered cuttingly.

Blair came closer, hands urging her to listen to his explanation. 'I know you don't want to hear this. I know you have every right to be hurt and angry, but there's no need to be. I may have lied in the past, even up to the time I went to the States, but something happened to me while I was gone, Sian. Something I should have seen coming a long time ago. In my pride, I was blind. Remember, you told me to look out. I should have listened. I couldn't believe just how much I missed you, Sian. I couldn't understand it—not until the truth hit me. I discovered I'd fallen in love with you.'

His head shot sideways at the force of her hand on his cheek. Even as he straightened up, the red weals were appearing.

'Liar!'

The only colour in Blair's face was the mark of her palm and the dark, troubled blue of his eyes. 'It isn't a lie,' he asserted thickly. 'I knew it then, and it was even clearer when I came back and saw you waiting for me. Before I left, I knew I was attracted to you, but I had sworn an oath to Neal and I was determined to carry it through. I never doubted I could and would do it. Then, when I realised just what my feelings were, I didn't know what to do. How could I love the woman who had driven Neal to his death? Who had tried to wriggle out of paying for it by every means she knew? Even to the point of inventing a totally unbelievable story!' He swallowed then with some difficulty. 'The truth was that I did— irreversibly. I thought—you gullible fool, you're just like Neal! That made me determined not to give way. Yet when I saw you again, I knew I just couldn't do it. I loved you and nothing else mattered. I believed that I could turn you into an honest woman because you loved me. I would cure you of all the lies you told.' Both look and voice were agonised. 'How could I have known it was all true?'

Sian bunched her hands into fists. 'It's called trust, Blair. It's part and parcel of loving!'

Blair winced. 'I know, but it was so hard.'

'It isn't supposed to be easy,' she scorned, eyes glittering with angry, desolate tears. 'You do it because you love someone.' Like she had loved him.

'I love you. I'll swear it on anything you care to name.'

Sian brushed the angry tears from her eyes with hands that trembled as violently as the rest of her. 'You could swear it on a whole stack of Bibles and I wouldn't believe you.'

He took an agitated step forwards. 'Sian...'

She reared away. 'Don't touch me! I couldn't bear you to touch me!' she said with loathing.

Hastily he stepped back again, hands raised placatingly. 'All right, calm down. I won't touch you. All I want is for you to listen to me.'

'What?' she laughed harshly. 'So you can tell me again about the picture and what it meant to you?' She had had time to work out that lie, too.

A nerve started to tick in his jaw. 'I'll admit there wasn't a picture. I had every intention of leading you on when I said that.'

Sian's trembling was turning to shaking in reaction. She had to clench every muscle to stop it from showing. 'What was your plan, Blair?'

Blair shook his head. 'There's no point in your knowing. For God's sake, don't throw this all away. I love you, and you love me. Don't make me hurt you.'

'When did you become so nice? You owe me honesty.'

Blair's eyes told of his deep frustration and helplessness. Yet she was right, he had to go on. 'As soon as I realised you loved me, I intended to lead you on to believe I loved you. Then I would have cast you off the way you did Neal,' he answered hoarsely, with painful truth.

'Dear God!' she cried, blanching. 'Dear God!'

His expression was tormented. 'But I changed my mind, Sian. I couldn't do it. I loved you, damn it. To hurt you is to hurt myself. Why won't you believe me?'

Her face was crumpling, breaking up into lines of pain. 'Because you lied to me. Because you broke my trust. All my life I've longed to have someone love me. *Really* love me. I thought it was Neal, but you know now what my father did to us. Then you came and gave me hope. I gave you everything without reservation, and you used it against me. How could you love me and still do that? I'll never forgive you!'

Blair threw caution to the winds and caught hold of her. 'How can you throw away everything there is between us?'

'Because it's dross! Worthless!' she cried, striving for freedom.

'But you love me,' he declared, fighting her efforts to break free. 'Don't be a fool!'

Desperately she dug her nails into his hands. 'I'd be a fool to stay here. Let me go.' At last she managed to break free, putting the width of the bed between them. Panting, she faced him. 'I'm leaving.'

Grimly, Blair took up a stance by the door. 'You're staying until I've made you see reason.'

Frustrated tears misted her eyes as she surveyed him, so full of grim purpose. She wanted to get out, to breathe freely again. She forced herself to calm down and think.

'OK, you won't let me go, so I'll have to listen. Only I have to use the bathroom first.'

He didn't attempt to stop her, though she felt his eyes on her. She went into the room, shut the door, turned on the tap and went straight out through the connecting door. It was simple then to go through the bedroom, on to the landing and across to the stairs. She had already started down them when Blair realised he had been tricked. She ran down, careless of life and limb, the sound of Blair's pursuit loud in her ears. The need to escape made her reckless when tears blurred her vision.

She darted across the hall, wrenched open the front door and fled into the night. Blair erupted after her, calling her name. She reacted like a nervous filly. Fear lent wings to her heels as she raced down the short drive and out on to the main road. Intent only on freedom, she slipped through the parked cars.

If Blair hadn't called her name, and if she hadn't faltered, maybe the car wouldn't have hit her. But he did call, and she did glance back, and in that instant she stepped from darkness into the path of the oncoming car. Winged, she was tossed violently backwards on to one of the parked vehicles, and from there rolled off it to the ground. By which time she was already blessedly unconscious.

The first time Sian opened her eyes, everything was red. Red as the pain that filled her and made her moan aloud. Someone came then and she felt the injection they gave her. She was conscious, too, of someone else holding her hand. Then the cool blackness returned.

The next time it happened, the pain was still there, only bearable, and her nose told her she was in hospital. It was a smell she disliked intensely. She moaned, and almost at once there was a friendly face peering down at her.

'Hello, so you're with us again. How do you feel? Are you in pain?'

Sian took a breath, or tried to, losing it as a sharp pain shot through her. She tried again. 'Not...bad... What...happened?'

The face smiled. 'You tried to argue with a car. Not something to be recommended.'

Sian tried to remember, but everything seemed so hazy. 'W...when?'

'Two days ago,' the face answered, taking her pulse. 'Your fiancé was here until a few hours ago. We had to send him home before he became another casualty. You're a popular young woman. The phone's been ringing off the wall with enquiries about you.'

Try as she might, Sian couldn't follow what she was being told, and the pain was growing again.

'Hurts,' she muttered, and very shortly another injection gave her the release she needed.

She had moments of wakefulness off and on after that, each time the interval longer and the pain less severe, until at last she surfaced without the really sharp pain in the background at all. She knew by now that she had broken her left arm and some ribs, and that she was practically all bruise. She had grazes too, so they told her, but that seemed nothing to the pain in her chest if she tried to take anything but shallow breaths.

Now she was awake, and it was evening, judging by the brightness of the electric light. And someone was holding her hand again. Twisting her head on the pillow, her eyes took in the sight of Blair slumped in a chair beside her. His eyes were closed and she thought he was asleep, until he must have sensed her gaze on him and his head came up.

Her heart jolted. He looked awful. There was no colour in his face at all, only lines of weariness and anxiety. His eyes were rimmed with purple shadows, their depths full of pain. She fought back the urge to comfort him.

'How do you feel?' he asked gently, his eyes watching carefully for a sign of pain.

'Like...I've been hit...by a car,' she whispered carefully.

'God!' Blair let her go and jumped to his feet, pacing to the window and back. 'It's no joke, Sian. I had to watch you tossed about like a rag doll!'

Sian watched him run a distracted hand around his neck. 'You should...have let me go.'

He went paler, if that was possible. 'We can't talk about that now. It can wait until you're better.'

'Nothing has...changed.'

His face tightened. 'Leave it, Sian. You're not supposed to get excited.'

She closed her eyes. 'Then go away.'

It was a dismissal, a permanent one. He knew it, but ignored it. 'I'll go and get some sleep, but I'll be back.'

Sian opened her eyes when she felt him leaning over her. He was going to kiss her and she didn't want that. She couldn't bear it. She turned her head swiftly and groaned at the jolt to her ribs.

Above her, Blair drew in a ragged breath, then dropped a kiss on her forehead. 'I love you,' he said in a low, husky voice. Then turned and left abruptly.

In the bed, Sian let the silent tears course down her face and tried to keep her breathing from turning into sobs. She wished the nurse would come and give her something to take away the pain, to give her oblivion. Not from her injuries, but from the mortal wound to her heart.

For the next few days she was too low to argue when Blair turned up to visit her. The only recourse she had was to turn her head away and try to ignore him. He must have known she didn't want him there, but he came anyway. He braved her silence with a stoicism that made her angry at her own inability to send him away. Was his skin so thick that he couldn't take a blunt hint? Worst of all, he always kissed her when he did eventually leave, and it tore her heart apart.

The healing process was slow. She graduated from lying to sitting by degrees. She could take stock of herself then, and it wasn't a pretty sight. Beneath the hospital gown she was all bruise—a Technicolor nightmare. Besides that, her hair needed washing, which made her irritable.

Into this mood, Blair brought his parents. The relief of not having to face him alone made her smile for the first time in days. Besides, she was genuinely pleased to see them.

Blair stood at the end of the bed as first Nancy and then Robert stooped to kiss her. He didn't attempt to do the same, which Sian could see puzzled his parents greatly. She glanced at him and saw the wry twist of his lips. He knew that if he had tried to kiss her, she would have turned away, and that sort of humiliation he didn't need. Sian felt an uncomfortable warmth invading her cheeks. Would she have behaved so childishly? She didn't know. Then she remembered the true state of affairs between them, and was damned if she would be made to feel the guilty one.

'My goodness, Sian!' Nancy said, taking the seat Blair usually occupied. 'You gave us all a nasty fright. What possessed you to run into the road like that?'

Sian looked down towards Blair, who instantly braced himself. 'Demons,' she said, and saw how his hands clenched into fists before he strode away to stand staring out of the window.

His parents exchanged speaking glances.

'Well, anyway,' Nancy patted Sian's hand, 'I'm glad you're feeling so much better. Are you?'

Sian managed a weak laugh. At the sound of it, over by the window, Blair held on tightly to the window-ledge.

'Yes,' Sian reassured. 'I came off lightly, considering. As they say, it only hurts when I laugh.'

'It's just as well you don't have much to laugh about,' Blair said bitingly, driven to it by her cheerfulness.

At once there were only the two of them there. 'You know how you can solve that problem,' she retorted.

He turned on her a face like stone. 'The answer is still no,' he ground out, and unceremoniously quit the room.

Sian squeezed back hot tears, realising that bitter exchange had been witnessed. 'I'm sorry about that,' she apologised shakily.

'Do you want me to leave you two alone?' Robert enquired tactfully.

Nancy sent him a smile. 'Yes, if you wouldn't mind, dear. Go and see if you can find Blair. I'll stay and keep Sian company.'

When Robert had gone, a silence fell. Sian pleated the sheet under her fingers and avoided looking at Nancy until she spoke.

'Do you want to tell me about it?'

'No,' she said wanly, but her eyes pleaded forgiveness. This was his mother. How could she possibly reveal what Blair had done?

Nancy sighed, sitting back, watching the girl in the bed thoughtfully. 'When Blair told us what had happened, he was in a dreadful state. I'd never seen him like it. When he continued to look so awful, I thought it was because you weren't doing too well. Now I see it's due to something else entirely. Something's eating away at him, making him dreadfully unhappy. If you know what it is, can't you tell me?'

Sian wanted to talk to someone, but how could she? What Blair had done was personal, it couldn't be allowed to harm his family. 'I'm sorry, I can't,' she replied unhappily.

'Can't, or won't?' Nancy probed with a touch of acerbity, and Sian flinched.

'If Blair has something on his conscience, then he must be the one to tell you. Although I wouldn't count on it,' Sian declared, wiping away the tears from her lashes.

At once Nancy leant forward to clasp the nervously moving fingers. 'Oh, I'm sorry, Sian. I can see it's hurting you too, whatever it is. I shouldn't have spoken like that. I will speak to Blair, because I hate to see you hurting each other like this. Now, cheer up, I've brought a bag of gifts here for you. Plus some nighties so you can get out of those dreadful hospital gowns.'

No more was said of the matter, but Blair didn't put in an appearance. Only Robert returned to say farewell. It was on the tip of Sian's tongue to ask if he was all right, but she suddenly felt overwhelmed by a sense of hypocrisy. She didn't care what happened to him, did she? His parents went, promising to visit again soon.

It was Sunday afternoon when Sian saw Blair again. She was sitting in a chair by the window, reading, when he walked in, casually dressed in jeans and sweater, and carrying a bunch of red roses. Seeing them, Sian pursed her lips.

'My feelings for you aren't going away, just because you won't accept them,' he said tautly.

He dropped the bouquet on the table and came to kiss her. As usual, Sian turned her head away, but this time exasperation got the better of Blair and he caught her chin in his hand and forced her round so that he could find her lips with his. Unable to fight, she refused to open them to him, and when he pulled back, she glared at him from bright eyes.

'Don't ever do that again.'

His lips twisted. 'If you won't give, I'll take.'

'That's about all I'd expect from a liar and a cheat.'

Blair sat down and rested one ankle on the other knee. His gaze was brooding. 'I can't deny that I set out to do both those things. But you can't deny that in the end I did neither.'

'Only because you were found out!' she snapped back.

He shifted, sitting forward to emphasise his point. 'I told you I'd already decided I couldn't go through with it. My God, I was scared out of my mind. Afraid of the very thing that is happening now. I had too damn much to lose,' he declared passionately, eyes challenging her to doubt it.

Tears flooded her eyes and her chest tightened. Why did he have to go on hurting her this way? 'You've lost it anyway.'

He shot to his feet. 'I refuse to accept that.'

'It's over, Blair. Take back your ring and get out of my life,' she ordered painfully.

He looked as if he would like to shake her. 'Why won't you forgive me?' he demanded gruffly.

He sounded as close to breaking as she had ever heard any man, and her throat closed over. 'Because I can't trust you. You looked at me with love in your eyes and it was all a lie. How can I ever know what you really feel and believe? In order to do that I have to trust you, and I can't do that because you've destroyed it.'

Blair stared at her distraught face, appalled by what she said. He had to swallow hard to remove a constriction from his throat. 'Then I have to make you trust me again, because I won't lose you now. Neither will I break the engagement, Sian. If nothing else, it binds you to me, and I'll use anything, anything at all to win you back,' he vowed huskily.

They faced one another, hurting as only people who love one another can be hurt.

'Get out,' Sian croaked at last. Then, stronger, 'Get out!' The effort to shout hurt her, and she cradled her arm across her chest.

Indecision was clear on Blair's face, yet her pain made it impossible for him to stay and argue.

'Very well,' he said. 'I'll go, but this isn't over.'

It is, it is, she told the door that closed behind him. She wouldn't let him hurt her any more. She climbed carefully to her feet and crossed to the bed, groping for the buzzer. The nurse who came in answer entered with a smile that immediately turned to a frown.

'What's up, love? Is something hurting you?' she queried in a light Irish brogue.

Only my heart, Sian thought silently.

'I want...I don't want...' she began agitatedly, groping for enough calm to add, 'I don't want to see Mr Davenport again. If he comes, you must send him away.'

'What, that darlin' man?' the nurse chided, sure this was just a lovers' tiff, for everyone knew the man was devoted to her.

Sian forced back a sob. 'If you think he's a darling, you're welcome to him. Can it be done?' she demanded, breathing heavily.

The nurse at last took her seriously. 'Now don't upset yourself, love. If that's what you want, then that's that. We'll do our best to keep him away.'

Sian sighed in relief. 'That's what I want,' she confirmed, but when the nurse left to sort the problem out, the tears wouldn't be denied.

Whether Blair tried to get in to visit her or not she didn't know, but she didn't see him for the rest of her stay in hospital. She had plenty of visitors. No one made any reference to Blair's absence, not even Nancy, who called in regularly. Sian knew she should have been happy. It was what she wanted, yet she worried.

Many times it was on the tip of her tongue to ask Nancy how he was, but always she thought better of it. The ambivalence of her emotions set her at war with herself. She *was* doing the right thing. Only a fool would lay themselves open to possible hurt. Yet the pricks of her conscience told her that nobody could guarantee not to hurt or be hurt.

What Blair had set out to do was reprehensible, and nothing could excuse that, even the fact that he hadn't carried it through to the end. How could he expect her to live with the knowledge of what he was capable of? She would never feel secure.

Why, then, was she still so unhappy?

Several days before she was due to leave hospital, Nancy paid her another visit. Sian realised at once that the older woman was uncomfortable about something, and it wasn't long before she discovered why.

'Sian, dear,' she began, choosing her words with care, 'I wouldn't ask this if I didn't feel it was important. Won't you change your mind and let Blair come and visit you? I promised myself I wouldn't interfere, but I can't stand to see my son, my strong son, looking so— so desolate. He took this ban very hard, you know.'

Sian couldn't look at her, for she had had a vision of the past and present mixed, where Blair became super-imposed on Neal. It shocked her, but she shook it off. Frowning, she stared through the window. 'Did Blair tell you why I did it?'

Nancy sighed. 'If you're asking me if I know what he was going to do, then yes, I do know. He was wrong to have even contemplated it. However, one fact does remain. He didn't love you at the beginning, but when he fell in love, carrying on with the plan was the last thing on his mind. He wouldn't hurt you for the world, Sian.'

'But he has,' she cried, turning an anguished face towards his mother.

Nancy reached out to clasp Sian's good hand. 'And he's hurting, too. It's tearing him apart that you won't let him near you. He loves you.'

Hot tears spilled from Sian's eyes. 'No, he doesn't.'

Nancy bit her lips. 'But why won't you believe him?'

It was a question she had asked herself many times, and the answer was clear. 'How could he come to love me so quickly after hating me?'

His mother took a deep breath and proceeded cautiously, 'Yet, in the same amount of time, you fell in love with someone who you knew hated you. Why should it be that with everything against him, you love him, if not because, deep down inside, you know he loves you?'

Sian had never looked at it like that. She bit her lip. 'How can I believe him?' she asked in a small voice, but really the question she was asking was, how could she ever again trust her own instincts and judgement if she didn't?

'That is the trusting part, Sian. If all he still wanted to do was humiliate you, then he could have done it a hundred times over.' Nancy sighed, and patted her hand. 'OK, I won't say any more. I can't force you to see him, but I do hope you will think about what I said. It isn't easy to trust, I know. Just don't do anything hasty that you might live to regret.'

They said no more on the subject, but Sian thought about it a lot in the next few days. Dared she believe he was speaking the truth when he said he loved her? He had said it over and over again, even though she refused to listen. He must have sunk his pride to do it and receive her continuous snubs. He was the one who was courting humiliation in order to get her to believe him. If it wasn't true, wouldn't he merely have given up?

She was tormented by doubts. Had she been wrong to condemn so quickly? Lord knew, she wanted to trust him, but dared she? This last question dogged her through sleepless nights. It would take an act of faith. Like taking that first parachute jump and trusting that it would open when the cord was pulled. Yet what good was trust if it needed proofs? How could he prove he loved her to her satisfaction? How could he believe she loved him, without the inherent trust? If she had to prove she loved him, what would she do?

She had answered her own question. There was nothing he could do, it was all up to her now. Either she loved and trusted him or she didn't. The two couldn't be separated. Yet while she accepted the truth of that, she also knew that she was more afraid than she had ever been in her life, of making that decision.

# CHAPTER TEN

SIAN was still avoiding making a decision when, the day before she expected to be released, the Davenports sprang a surprise on her. Nancy and Robert insisted she must come back home to them to continue her convalesence.

This, on top of her thoughts, was too much. Her cheeks grew hot. 'Oh, but I couldn't!' she protested, glancing from one to the other by turns.

'If you're worried about Blair, don't be. It was his suggestion,' Robert informed her.

'Oh!' Surprise made her colour deepen. Then she swallowed nervously. 'H-how is he?'

Nancy drew a quick breath, then said swiftly, 'Well, dear, naturally he isn't the life and soul of the party, but he seems to be coping.'

Coping? That sounded awful, and Sian felt her chest become tight. 'I don't see how you can be so kind to me when...' She couldn't bring herself to say more, only looking anxiously at them.

'Because we think you and Blair were made for each other. You both know it, too. We're trying to help you. If we didn't think you had a future together, we would cut the cord to be kind,' Nancy said huskily. Robert's hand on her shoulder underlined his agreement.

Sian bit her lip to stop the ready tears from falling. Crying was all she seemed able to do these days. 'Then thank you, I will come. And...' She hesitated.

'And?' Robert prompted, smiling fondly at her.

She took a deep breath. 'I have been thinking—about what you said.'

Nancy squeezed her hand. 'I'm pleased, dear. And have you...?' She left the sentence unfinished.

Sian lifted one shoulder diffidently. 'I don't know.'

Standing up, Nancy bent to kiss Sian's cheek. 'Well, that's something, at least. Now, Robert and I shall be here bright and early to collect you. Blair sent a whole load of your things on to the house, so you needn't worry on that score. All that you will be required to do is heal.'

When they left, Sian lay back against her pillows. Blair wanted her to go home with his parents. Her heart skipped and took on a new rhythm. He was offering her the balm of loving concern that should have been his, when he needed it every bit as much as she did. As that thought registered, her heart was assailed by a barrage of emotions, but chiefly love and anxiety. She cared about him, and she couldn't do that without loving him. Loving meant trusting.

She had been punishing him, but that had gone on long enough. Hurting him further meant hurting herself too, just as he had once said to her. She knew then that she had to see him, to tell him that she was willing to try again. A relationship founded on so many misconceptions and mistakes had been bound to falter. This time they must start fresh, with nothing hidden. That way she knew they could make it work.

She was glad now that she had decided to stay with the Davenports. Blair was sure to turn up within a day or two. She strongly suspected he had made the suggestion because she couldn't ban him from the house as she had the hospital. It was just the devious sort of thing he would do.

Only he didn't come. She waited and waited in a growing, sick despair. She had hurt him too much and left it too late. He had done what she had told him she wanted, and walked out of her life.

That realisation made her crushingly aware, if she had needed it, that that was the only thing she was certain she didn't want. She loved him and needed him. Without him, there was simply no colour in the world. She couldn't talk about it to anyone. She knew that, although they wouldn't say it, she deserved their 'I told you so'.

She tried phoning the apartment, but could only get the answering machine, and hung up without leaving a message. The only thing she could think of to do was wait until she went back to work—presuming, by then, she would still have a job to go to.

She tried to be positive. If she could see him, she was sure she could convince him to change his mind again. That certainty kept her spirits up during the worst moments when dejection threatened to get the better of her.

Late one evening, when she was in the kitchen making coffee, having volunteered because Mrs Murray had already retired, the door to the hall swished open and closed again. Thinking it was one of the others come to help, she turned with a smile which froze when she came face to face with Blair.

Shock kept her stock-still, but her heart, after one anxious lurch, ran on at a tremendous rate. She was unbelievably pleased to see him, but the changes in him! Her eyes, eager to take in this unlooked-for feast, widened in dismay, and she couldn't quite hold back a gasp. He looked as if a smile would crack his face. What tan he had had was gone, and he looked muddy with fatigue and disheartenment.

Slowly the colour drained from her face. He looked so miserable! 'I didn't hear you arrive,' was all she could manage to say in a flat voice. Her eyes strayed to his shirt and jeans. Her heart ached. They no longer hugged him lovingly as she remembered.

Grim amusement flickered in the depths of Blair's eyes as he walked further into the room. 'Don't worry, I won't be staying long.'

Realising in shock how he had misinterpreted her remark, she stumbled into speech. 'I didn't mean to imply you weren't welcome.'

'However, we both know it's true,' he added drily.

'I haven't kept you away from here, Blair. You could have come any time,' she told him quietly, feeling as if there was an invisible six-foot wall between them.

He afforded her a smile that carried a lot of his old mocking quality. 'Masochism doesn't happen to be one of my hobbies.'

Sian flushed painfully. 'I never meant to drive you away from your home.' Lord, why was she saying everything but what was really important?

Blair sighed and rubbed his hand round his neck in a curiously defeated gesture. 'You didn't. I wanted you to come here. I didn't fancy the idea of you being on your own.'

'It was very kind of you to suggest it, under the circumstances,' she thanked him uncomfortably.

He eyed her with a quirky smile that didn't reach his eyes. 'We're being polite, aren't we?'

They were, and she didn't like it one little bit. Yet she didn't know how to break it. 'I was making coffee. Do you want some?' she asked stiffly.

'Thanks.' He hooked out a chair with his foot and sat down at the table, watching her move about the kitchen. 'You're looking well.'

She threw him a smile. 'Your family have been looking after me almost too well.'

'I suppose that means you'll be leaving soon,' he declared, accepting the cup she handed him, ostentatiously avoiding touching her in any way.

Sian bit her lip at the subtle manoeuvre and sat down opposite him. 'Soon,' she agreed.

Blair sipped at the refreshing liquid with enjoyment. 'I needed that.'

Concern clouded her eyes. 'You look tired. Have you been working too hard?'

He flexed his neck and shoulders expressively. 'There's no such thing as too hard. It's amazing what you can do if you set your mind to it.'

She knew what he meant. He had been using work to keep from thinking. Once, she had done the same thing herself. But she had been self-driven. This was something she had forced on him.

'That's no solution,' she chastised him.

Blue eyes flashed. 'Do you have another suggestion?' he demanded bleakly, and she flinched.

'I have been doing a lot of thinking,' she told him, swallowing nervously, trying to feel her way into telling him how she felt.

His eyes narrowed. 'And?'

'I don't know...' she began, but he didn't allow her to finish.

The cup went back into the saucer with a crash. 'Will you ever know, do you think?' He caught her surprise, and misinterpreted it. 'Oh, yes, I've been getting reports from my mother. She seems to be under the impression you will come out on my side. Well, I'm not a prize waiting to be picked up. I won't wait around for you for ever. The choice is simple. Either you believe me or you don't. You were merciful with Neal, so it's the very least you can give me.'

'I'm trying to tell you...' she tried again, but he broke in once more.

His look was vicious. 'Oh, yes, I know. You're just avoiding the issue. Which means your choice is obvious, and makes it easy for me to make the decision for you. It's over. You've won. The freedom you want so badly is yours.'

Blair stood up as he finished, and Sian followed his movements with disbelieving eyes. It took for ever for her paralysed brain to accept the fact that he was actually leaving, and when he walked through the door, everything she wanted, everything she loved and needed, would go with him.

'No!' she called out after him, coming to her feet.

He halted and half turned towards her. 'Yes,' he returned firmly.

Her face set mutinously. 'But I love you, and I don't want you to go.'

His chest rose as he took a deep breath. 'And I love you, but I have to go.'

She hadn't thought it could be so hard to convince him. 'Why?'

'Because it seems to be the only way to prove to you that I love you,' he told her, his face pale and strained. 'So it's goodbye, Sian.' He continued on his way.

Anger and dismay galvanised her into action. 'Don't you dare give up without a fight, Blair Davenport! If you walk through the door I'll never forgive you,' she cried out after him, and underlined it with the first object that came to hand.

Blair turned in time to duck the first cup and dodge the saucer. 'Are you crazy?' he snapped furiously.

'No, just desperate,' she retorted, letting fly.

A badly aimed tea-plate caught him a stinging blow on the shin. He swore and backed off a step, holding up his hands.

'Why are you so angry? I've done what you wanted.'

Another cup took wing. 'No, you haven't. If you're going to make up my mind for me, at least make it up the right way!' she declared angrily, launching the sugar bowl.

He was so much surprised, he almost forgot to duck. He did so in time, and received a shower of granules which he shook off like a dog.

'Are you saying you believe me?' he demanded, crunching forwards over a layer of china.

She took a flying leap into space, gripping that parachute release cord. 'Yes,' she said, and started counting.

Still he came forward. 'And you forgive me?'

'Yes.' Still counting.

'Then do you mind telling me why you're so angry?' He was no more than a yard away.

Sian armed herself with the cream jug. 'I have a right to be for what you did, don't I?'

'You do,' he admitted ruefully, coming to a halt and eyeing the next missile warily. 'You're not going to throw that.'

She pulled the cord and waited. 'I will if necessary.'

Suddenly he began to look amused. 'If I come up with the wrong answer? OK, I'm staying. Not because you demand it, but because I love you very much and have done so for ever.'

The parachute opened and she floated. It was the cream jug that landed with a crash. She didn't hear it, for by then she was firmly caught in Blair's arms. It was like coming home after being lost in the wilderness for years. Everything was in that first kiss, the hands that strove so desperately to hold each other closer. The anger, the pain, the forgiveness—and the love.

The family, who had come to investigate the sounds of destruction, withdrew tactfully, consoling Nancy on the loss of her second-best coffee-set. Which was totally irrelevant, as she would have sacrificed anything for the pleasure of seeing Blair and Sian together where they belonged.

In the kitchen, Sian eased herself away from him, 'Did you do that on purpose?' she asked huskily.

His smile was tender. 'You mean, say I was leaving? No. I wish I had thought of it. All I knew was that I couldn't go on like this any longer. Both of us were miserable, and I held the answer in my hands. I couldn't remain selfishly holding on. I loved you, and what you wanted mattered. I had to let you go.'

Her hands went up around his head again, and she pressed her cheek to his. 'I didn't mean to make you so terribly unhappy,' she apologised in a low voice.

He held her close, almost convulsively. 'As I never wanted to hurt you. Are you sure you forgive me?'

'I'm sure. I doubted you because I was hurt, and then I was too scared to trust you again. Only, I realised I still loved you. Which I couldn't do if you weren't the man I thought you to be. And where I love, I trust.' Sian pulled away so she could see him. 'I do love you, Blair.'

His incredibly blue eyes carried a dizzying message, and the whole of his face had lost years. 'Thank you. That's all I could ever want from this world.'

They came together in a kiss that left them flushed and breathless. Reluctantly they drew apart, and as they moved their feet crunched on the debris of their battle-field and they looked down in consternation.

'Oh, dear!' Sian was swamped by a wave of guilt at the destruction. 'Do you think they still make this design? We ought to replace it.'

Blair agreed, but with a broad grin on his face. 'I suppose we ought to clear it up. You know, you bowl a mean googly. Ever thought of taking it up professionally?'

'Oh, don't!' she groaned, once again realising where her red hair had led her.

Between the two of them it didn't take long to remove all signs of the recent conflict.

'Do you think we ought to make some more coffee for them?' she suggested as Blair draped an arm about her shoulders and steered her out to the hall.

'If we go in there, we'll have to stay, and I'd rather be alone with you for now,' he answered, his eyes running over her hotly.

At the foot of the stairs they stopped.

'I don't think we're expected, anyway,' he added as he picked up the bottle of champagne and two glasses left in the middle of one of the stairs. 'My father can be quite embarrassingly blunt at times. However, I can't fault him on the idea. Let's go up. I want to drink a toast to the woman I love.'

In her room he quickly poured two glasses, handing one to her. 'To us—may we always be as happy as we are right now.'

'To us,' she responded, and their eyes locked as they drank.

'Neal would be happy, I think,' she said later, as they sat side by side on the bed.

Blair's face clouded over. 'I wish I'd never started on that fool stunt. It caused us too much pain and wasted so much time.'

Sian set down her glass and slipped her arms round him. 'I shudder to think how close I came to losing you. I was a fool.'

Disposing of his own glass, Blair eased her down against the pillows, smoothing the dark red tendrils of hair from her cheeks. 'No, you weren't, my darling. I hurt you badly, when all I wanted to do was protect you from pain. You really ought not to forgive me so easily.'

Sian smiled, a sight full of wondrous grace and beauty, that encompassed the whole of her feelings for him. 'Yet I do, because I love you,' she said softly.

Blair caught his breath. 'I don't deserve this, but I'm going to grasp it with both hands and never let go.'

Sapphire eyes held his as she slid her arms up around his neck. 'I love you,' she said again.

A smile began to grow on Blair's face, too. 'Is that all you're going to say?' he asked, his rich voice incredibly husky.

Sian shook her head. 'I love you.' Her arms began to exert pressure, pulling his head down until his lips almost brushed hers.

Blair groaned, tantalised. 'Will you marry me as soon as it can be arranged?'

This time she nodded. 'I love you,' she sighed against his mouth.

With a low laugh, Blair succumbed. 'A woman with a three-word vocabulary—what a novel idea.'

He couldn't say any more because she was kissing him, and then he was kissing her, until finally they were kissing each other. Then, some time later, he lifted his head and murmured a husky, 'I love you.' As far as vocabulary went, three words were enough.

# H A R L E Q U I N
## *Romance*

## Coming Next Month

Available in March wherever paperback books are sold, or through Harlequin Reader Service:

In the U.S.
901 Fuhrmann Blvd.
P.O. Box 1397
Buffalo, N.Y. 14240-1397

In Canada
P.O. Box 603
Fort Erie, Ontario
L2A 5X3

## The Pirate
### JAYNE ANN KRENTZ

At the heart of every powerful romance story lies a legend. There are many romantic legends and countless modern variations on them, but they all have one thing in common: They are tales of brave, resourceful women who must gentle and tame the powerful, passionate men who are their true mates.

The enormous appeal of Jayne Ann Krentz lies in her ability to create modern-day versions of these classic romantic myths, and her LADIES AND LEGENDS trilogy showcases this talent. Believing that a storyteller who can bring legends to life deserves special attention, Harlequin has chosen the first book of the trilogy—THE PIRATE—to receive our Award of Excellence. Look for it now.

AE-PIR-1A

February brings you . . .

# Harlequin Presents...

Award of Excellence

# PENNY JORDAN

## valentine's night

*Sorrel didn't particularly want to meet her
long-lost cousin Val from Australia. However,
since the girl had come all this way just to
make contact, it seemed a little churlish not to
welcome her.*

*As there was no room at home, it was agreed
that Sorrel and Val would share the Welsh
farmhouse that was being renovated for
Sorrel's brother and his wife. Conditions were
a bit primitive, but that didn't matter.*

*At least, not until Sorrel found herself snowed
in with the long-lost cousin, who turned out to
be a handsome, six-foot male!*

Also, look for the next Harlequin Presents
Award of Excellence title in April:

### Elusive as the Unicorn
### by Carole Mortimer

HP1243-1